A Papa Like Everyone Else

A Papa
Like
Everyone Else

Follett Publishing Company
1010 West Washington Boulevard
Chicago, Illinois 60607

Sydney Taylor

Illustrated by George Porter

Follett Publishing Company

CHICAGO NEW YORK

ACM

Library of Congress Catalog Number: AC 66-16942

FIRST PRINTING

Follett Publishing Company
1010 West Washington Boulevard
Chicago, Illinois 60607

T/L-6725

GERTRUDE

*To her memory
And her memories*

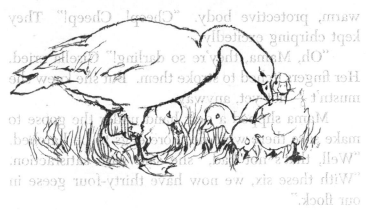

ONE

GISELLA sat very still, her pale green eyes round with wonder. Again the miracle was happening! She had seen it many times before, but always her pulse quickened with the mystery of it.

Pick — pick! An egg under the mother goose cracked. Gisella could see the tiny yellow beak pecking through.

"Szerena!" she called to her sister, "Come quick!"

Szerena strolled over and sat down beside her. Together they watched the wee bodies struggling out from the smooth white walls that had imprisoned them for so long. Soon, six wet, bedraggled baby goslings were wriggling under their mother's warm, protective body. "Cheep! Cheep!" They kept chirping excitedly.

"Oh, Mama, they're so darling!" Gisella cried. Her fingers itched to stroke them. But she knew she mustn't — not yet, anyway.

Mama slipped a deft hand under the goose to make sure there were no more eggs to be hatched. "Well, that's not bad," she said with satisfaction. "With these six, we now have thirty-four geese in our flock."

The big wall oven was sending waves of heat throughout the front room. Gradually the down on the baby geese dried, and they were transformed into round yellow balls of fluff.

Mama put a small pan of water before the straw mat. Making a clucking sound, she coaxed the babies to drink. But they did not know how. Gently, she pushed the little round beaks into the pan. After a few tries, they began to sip, throwing their heads back comically as the water ran down their gullets.

Gisella picked up one of the yellow balls, cupping it tenderly in her hands. She held it to her face, brushing the downy softness against her cheek. "Oh, you darling, darling!" she cooed, kissing it. A small globule of saliva glistened on her lips. Instantly the baby goose sipped at it.

Gisella giggled. "It's kissing me!"

"Silly," Szerena said matter-of-factly. "It's just learned how to drink. It saw the spit on your lip, so it drank, that's all."

But Gisella was quite sure that the gosling really had kissed her.

"It's time the little things had their first meal," Mama said. She mixed some fine grits with water in a pan and set it down on the floor. The goose rose, ruffled her feathers, and headed straight for the pan, the goslings wobbling anxiously after her. As she hovered over the pan, she kept turning and looking at her children. Watch me, then do as I do, she seemed to be saying.

She stretched her neck downward, pecking at the grits with her beak. Then she deposited some on the floor beside her chirping brood. The babies nipped at the food gingerly. It must have tasted good, for in no time, they were hopping up and down trying to get into the pan.

Meanwhile, Szerena had cleared away the messy nest. In its place, Mama set a big wooden box with a sievelike bottom, and when the goslings had finished their meal, she put them all into the box. Their mother jumped in after them. She spread her wings wide, and the little round fluffs tumbled over one another trying to get close to her.

For several days, Mama kept the brood in the house. Then one morning she said to Gisella, "Now they're ready to go for a stroll."

Gisella held out her pinafore, and carefully, one by one, Mama put in the baby geese. Walking with cautious steps so as not to jostle them, Gisella

9

stepped across the ledge of the house. Behind her trailed their mother, honking worriedly.

It was a bright, sunny day. White clouds, looking freshly laundered, were sailing across a sky of deep blue. The morning sun was already suspended like a crown of pale gold. The yellow dandelions dotting the new spring grass, seemed to be nodding in gay greeting.

Gisella knelt down, releasing her hold on her pinafore, and the little ones came tumbling out. In a confused huddle, they poked about, chirping furiously at everything. They look just like the dandelions, only bigger, she thought.

While the mother hovered near, the babies began nibbling at the grass. Gisella laughed as she watched them yanking at the sturdy blades of grass.

"What's so funny?" Szerena asked from the door.

"Just look at them! It's the first time they've ever seen grass. How do they know it's good for them?"

Szerena shrugged. "I guess God made them to know. Stop fussing with them, and go feed the other geese and chickens." She thrust a large pan of feed into Gisella's hands. "And don't take forever. You have to help me clean up, you know. Mama wants to get to the fields."

Gisella trudged toward the barn calling loudly, "Here chicky, chicky! Here goosey, goosey!" From everywhere the fowl came running, cir-

10

cling around her, clucking and cackling expectantly. Gisella scooped up fistfuls of the feed and tossed it to the impatient birds. She loved the smooth, mushy feeling of it slipping through her fingers. The fowl scattered about, pouncing on the morsels. Immediately, they were back for more, some of them even pecking at her toes. "You greedy things!" she scolded. "Mind your manners!"

In no time, the pan was empty. Gisella started back toward the house when suddenly, from afar, there came the sound of drum beats. "The *dobos!* The *dobos* is coming!" she shouted, dropping the pan with a clatter. She ran through the small garden, unlocked the wooden gate, and dashed out into the dirt road with Szerena close behind.

Rat-tat-tat! Rat-tat-tat! The drum sounded nearer! Now, even Mama wiped her hands on her apron, forsook her kitchen, and came on the run.

Up ahead, they could see the drummer turning into their street. "I hope he's bringing good news today!" Mama exclaimed.

Rat-tat-tat! Rat-tat-tat! Left, right, left, right! The drummer's short legs thrust forward. Behind him thronged the children of the village.

The *dobos* stationed himself right in front of Mama's house. His drum fell silent. The grown-ups and children gathered around, all attention. Taking out a sheaf of paper from his vest pocket, he cleared his throat importantly and began to read aloud. "There is sickness in the Kozma house. The child

Juli is down with scarlet fever. This is very contagious. Be sure to stay away and also keep your children away until the sickness is over."

There were murmurs of sympathy for the Kozmas.

The *dobos* continued. "The tax on the glass windows in your houses is due this week. I wish to remind you that it is one koruna for each window, and it is to be paid to the *biro* (judge) this week."

"The main road at the railroad crossing needs repairs." The *dobos* paused, scanning the list before him. "The following people from this street are to report at the crossing tomorrow morning at 7 o'clock, ready for work. Janos Bacsi and Rezi Neni it is your turn now." He peered over the top of the paper at Mama. "Aunt Rezi your name is on the list, but I know you have no man to do this work for you. You will have to pay or get someone else to do it for you."

"I know," Mama said quietly. "I will speak to our neighbor's son, Imre. I will pay him to do the work."

"Good. And my final news is also for you Rezi Neni. There is a registered letter for you at the post office. You will have to go there to sign for it. It's from America."

"From my husband!" Mama cried.

The neighbors nodded and smiled to one another. "From America!" they echoed. "From her husband!"

12

Gisella heard the catch in Mama's voice. She could see the sudden joy lighting up Mama's tired face. Szerena, too, was all smiles. "I'll go with you, Mama," she said.

"Gisella, you gather up the goslings while we're gone," Mama called over her shoulder, as she and Szerena started for the post office.

Rat-tat-tat! Rat-tat-tat! The *dobos* marched off to the next street with the children prancing along.

Dutifully Gisella guided the chirping goslings back to their box. I'm glad for Mama and Szerena, she thought. I ought to be glad for myself, too. It's good to know I have a papa like everyone else, even if I only know about him from letters. A deep current of resentment stirred within her, sweeping aside all the happiness of the morning. She felt all mixed up. It's been so long since we heard from Papa, she mused. I had almost forgotten about him. It's all your fault, she railed mutely at the departed *dobos*. Did you have to come and tell us there was a letter? We were getting along just fine — the three of us — without any papa!

She sat down on the mat beside the box and fondled the little goslings. This gave her a measure of comfort against the unhappiness tugging at her.

Soon Mama and Szerena were back. Gisella rose and followed them into the big room, and they all sat down at the table. Slowly Mama turned the letter over in her work-worn hands. Then she laid it down before her, staring at it. If only she could read or write. Her fingers traced the address as the girls bent forward examining the strange stamp. Finally she tore open the envelope and gave the letter to Szerena. "Read!" she said. Hands folded in her lap, she leaned against the back of her chair watching the movement of her elder daughter's lips.

My dearest Wife,

I know it has been a long time since you heard from me. You must be thinking that I have forgotten all about my family. Never think that! I did not write because I felt you have enough to worry about taking care of the farm and the children all by yourself. I could not add to your troubles by telling you what happened to me.

"Oh!" Mama's hand flew to her cheek. Szerena stopped reading and glanced at her. "Go on! Read, read!" Mama cried anxiously.
Szerena continued.

Near the end of the war a very contagious sickness spread throughout America — influenza they call it. Thousands came down with it. It was a terrible epidemic and many died. In fact it is said that more people died of influenza than were killed in the war. But after a while the epidemic seemed to

14

let up. Those of us who had managed not to catch it were considered very lucky. Last winter there were still some cases but nothing alarming. Then suddenly I too was stricken and had to be rushed to the hospital. I had a very bad case. But God was with me. The crisis passed and I began to recover. It has taken over three months, but now, thank God, I am entirely well.

All that time when I lay ill, I might have had someone else write for me. But then you would have found out that I was in the hospital, and I did not want you to know. But now all this is past. I feel strong again and am back at work. Only it is a misfortune that the sickness used up so much of my savings.

It hasn't been easy to save. Since the war ended, the situation has been very unsettled here. Business isn't too good. There are many people without work. And prices for everything keep going up and up.

But everyone feels this is all part of getting back to normal after a war. Already I think there are signs that things will get better. So with God's help, I am praying that the day of our being together will not be too long away.

You will find in this letter a money order for $15.00. I wish it could be more. I know how much you need it. Now that I am back

15

at work I will try to send you something regularly.

It is very lonely here without you. I miss you and the children very much. How grownup they must be by now! God bless and keep you all.

$$\text{Your loving husband}$$
$$\text{Herschel}$$

Mama took the letter from Szerena, refolded it carefully, and slipped it back into the envelope. She walked over to the big, shiny black chest which stood by the bed near the window, lifted the lid, and drew out a small packet of letters. Untying the string, she placed the new letter on top and retied the bundle. When she turned to the girls, her eyes were filled with tears.

"You see how hard Papa is trying for us? And now he's sent us all this money. Thank God he came through the terrible sickness!" She smoothed back the graying hair from her forehead. "Szerena, you must write Papa tonight and tell him not to worry so much about us." She stood up briskly. "I've got to get to the fields. Szerena, you and Gisella finish straightening up the house, then come and help me." Tying a paisley kerchief around her head, she went out.

Gisella moved about the house quietly helping Szerena. They were spreading the bright red coverlet over the high box bed when suddenly she burst

16

out. "Szerena, what was Papa like?"

"I don't know, Gisella. It's been so long. I was only five when he left." Szerena's brown eyes seemed to be looking backward in time. "But I do know I loved him very much. I remember he used to pick me up and swing me around. I thought he was so big and strong!" She smiled. "He had a moustache, and when he kissed me, it tickled."

Her face grew pensive as she slowly summoned fragments from the past. "Papa had a deep down voice. When I sat in his lap, I could hear it rumbling in his chest. . . . He was always so gay . . . he used to laugh a lot . . . Mama did, too, in those days. . . ." She regarded Gisella thoughtfully. "I think about him often. But when I do, I get kind of confused. I don't know if what I think is something I actually remember or something that Mama has told me."

"Well, it doesn't seem right!" Gisella exploded. "He shouldn't have gone off and left us! With me just a baby only a year old!" Tears of self-pity dimmed her eyes. She bent her head, and her blond braids swung disconsolately forward.

"But, Gisella, there wasn't enough money for all of us to go. Besides, Papa thought it would be best if he went over first, got himself a job, and found a place for us to live. He wasn't the only man in the villages around here to do that. Mama said many husbands went away for a couple of years. Then when they were settled and had enough money, they sent for their families. It was just our hard luck that Papa left Hungary in 1914. He couldn't know that the war would break out that very year. And then all through the war, he couldn't get out, and we couldn't get in."

Szerena shook her head. "How many times during those dreadful years I used to wish we were with Papa in America. You were so little, Gisella. You haven't any idea how hard it was. Lucky for us there wasn't any actual fighting here in our village. But there were times when we could hear the guns thundering in the distance, and we would be terrified!

"And, of course, the army had to be fed. So naturally it was the farmers who had to supply the food. The government allowed us to keep our cow and some of our chickens and geese, but they kept taking away all the eggs and milk, butter and cheese. Even the good wheat that we raised had to be turned over, and they gave us some horrible flour instead. The bread that Mama made from it tasted awful. You used to cry, because you said you couldn't swallow it — it was as dry as sawdust. And we didn't have a drop of sugar. And all our fruit and vegetables — everything — everything that we grew had to go to the army.

"And always there were soldiers going through our village. All kinds — Hungarian, Czech, Russian. They had to sleep somewhere, so we had to put them up in our houses and give them food to eat, even though we ourselves were hungry." She gave a little shudder.

"And where was Papa all this time?" Gisella insisted stubbornly. "Nice and comfortable in America. Why didn't he help?"

"He did try to help us," Szerena replied. "He sent packages and money. But in wartime, mail is slow and uncertain. Once a whole year went by without hearing a single word from him." She sighed. "Somehow we managed. Maybe because there was always the hope that someday we'd be able to get to America."

Gisella smacked the plump down pillows into place. "Why does everyone want to go to America anyway? People should stay in their own country."

"Maybe so, but what is our country?" Szerena cried. "Before the war, we were part of the Austro-Hungarian Empire. Then when the war ended in 1918, they didn't even stop fighting here for another two years. Then they went and split the country up into many pieces. Don't you remember when everybody had to take down the picture of the Emperor and all the flags? Now you see only Czech flags. We speak Hungarian and we feel Hungarian, but now they say we are Czechoslovakians!"

"But that's all over now," Gisella ventured. "And I like it here. We still have our friends — and the farm — and this little house — and everything." Her eyes roamed around the room. It was always so bright and cheerful. Szerena had thrown open all three windows. The early spring air stirred the gay red flowered curtains, splashing their vivid color against the whitewashed walls. The sun's rays streamed through, shimmering along the smooth brown surfaces of dresser, table, and chairs. "It's so nice here," she added.

Szerena shook her head again. "No, Gisella, you're too young to understand. It's not all that wonderful. We have to work very hard for everything. Look at Mama. She's not so old. But she's always so tired and worried about money. And all the taxes we have to pay. If it weren't for the money and clothes that Papa sends us from time to time, I don't know how we'd get by. And it'll never be any different for us as long as we stay here, no matter how hard we try."

"I can understand how Papa felt," she went on. "Mama told me once that Papa was very unhappy here. He hated having to work from early morning till late at night for such a poor living. But what chance did he have to do anything else here?"

"Papa says that in America everyone has a chance to make something of himself. The schools there are free! Can you imagine!"

Gisella's mouth turned down. "But maybe we won't like it there," she argued. "Maybe we won't be happy. And we are happy here."

"Mama isn't," Szerena returned. "It's just too hard for her with no husband to help her. And besides, she's very lonesome without Papa."

A stab of jealousy pricked Gisella. "But she has us. We help a lot."

"It's not the same, Gisella. A wife needs her husband as well as her children. Just like children need a papa as well as a mama."

Gisella turned away. But I don't need him, she raged inwardly. And he doesn't really need us. If he did, he would have found some way to have us with him long before this. He could have sold the farm and the house and everything. Then maybe he would have had enough money. No! I'm sure he didn't want us! Well, now I don't want him! I'm very happy right here with Mama. With Mama and Szerena!

TWO

THE CLAPPER BELL pealed. Quickly the children gathered up their slates, their pens, ink bottles, and copybooks. As soon as the teacher had stationed himself at the door, they rose and chorused, *"Jo Napot Kivanok"* (I wish you a good day). Then, filing past him, two by two, they paraded sedately in two straight lines down the village street. School was over for the day.

I wonder what Mama will bring me this time, Gisella found herself thinking as she marched along. Early that morning Mama had set out for the city. Gisella had watched her walking away from the house, her slender body tipped forward with the weight of the heavy basket on each arm. In each basket lay a live goose covered with a clean white cloth. The birds were so big and fat, that their legs stuck out stiffly over the sides of the baskets.

When the marchers came by Mrs. Tulipan's house, they observed her busily tending her vegetable garden. "*Jo Napot Kivanok,* Mimi Neni," they greeted in unison, bowing politely.

Mrs. Tulipan smiled and waved to them. "*Isten Veletek*" (God be with you) she replied.

The line thinned out as the children reached their own streets. Gisella's thoughts returned to the geese. I hope Mama gets a lot of money for them. She worked hard fattening them up. It was way back in February when Mama had picked them out from the flock and brought them squawking indignantly into the house. She had fixed up a small pen in the front room, covered the earthen floor with fresh straw, and put the geese inside. "There!" she remembered Mama saying to the birds, "no more running around for you two. Here you stay until you're ready for market."

Mama force-fed each goose several times a day. First she sat down on a mat on the floor with a big goose in her lap. Then, with her right leg holding the goose firmly, she pried open its mouth and stuffed cornmeal mush into its throat. Gisella could see the lumps sliding down the goose's gullet. It made a gurgling sound as it swallowed.

At first, the geese didn't like being forced to eat. But they soon got used to it. After a while, they just lay around, too full from over-feeding to even stir. Only yesterday Szerena had cried, "Mama, these geese are so fat, they look like they'll burst!"

Mama looked pleased. "Yes, they're a fine pair. Whoever gets them is sure to have some nice liver. And there'll be plenty of rich, white fat, too."

By now the dwindling line of children had approached Gisella's house. She and Szerena stepped out and skipped through their own gate.

"Mama!" Gisella called out, but there was no answer.

"I guess she's not home yet," Szerena said.

Gisella waltzed about impatiently. "Oh, I wish Mama would hurry! I can't wait to see what she's bringing us."

"She told us already," reminded Szerena. "Material for our new dresses."

"Oh, I don't mean that. I mean — you know — something special — a treat!"

Gisella plopped her things down on the long bench. "Do you remember last autumn when the peddler came, Szerena? He had a box of shiny pins and buttons and pretty necklaces. Do you remember he said we could pick out something in exchange for the old iron and rags Mama saved up for him? Or if we'd rather, he'd give us a big bowlful of fresh cherries instead?"

"Uh-huh. I remember. We took the cherries. "Umm, mmm!"

24

"They were good. But they got eaten up so fast. And then we had nothing left but pits. We should have picked something from that box. Then we would have had something that lasted."

Szerena scoffed, but Gisella ignored her and went on. "There was a string of blue beads. They were so pretty. Next time the peddler comes, I'm going to ask Mama if I can choose beads."

"Come on," suggested Szerena, picking up her crocheting, "let's wait outside."

As they went through the front room, Gisella glanced at the pen. "It looks so empty without the geese," she remarked.

"Don't worry. There'll soon be others to take their place."

Szerena seated herself on the wide porchlike wooden platform jutting out from the front of the house. Soon her needle was devouring the thread with amazing speed. For a while, Gisella sat beside her, scanning the road. But she grew restless. Running down the path, she began swinging on the gate. Sq-ue-ek! Sq-ue-e-ek! The hinges creaked as she rode back and forth. Finally she cried out, "We could listen for the train."

Szerena put her crocheting down. "All right, fidgety," she said.

Hand in hand, the sisters walked to the rear of the house and through the vegetable garden. They crossed the field where the bare brown earth was already dotted with tender clumps of grass. Beyond lay the railroad tracks. Standing tiptoe on the ties, they peered into the distance. No train in sight. They knelt down and pressed their ears against the cold rail. Minutes dragged by. At last they could feel the rail begin to vibrate and hear the steady singing of the metal.

"It's coming!" Gisella yelled, springing up excitedly. "The train's coming! Let's run to the station!"

"No," Szerena said. "We'd better get back to the house."

The waiting seemed endless, but just when Gisella felt she could bear it no longer, there was Mama striding toward them. They raced up the road to greet her.

"Mama!" they cried, covering her with embraces.

"Was it a good day?" Szerena asked.

"Yes. Very good." Mama looked weary, but her face was all smiles. "Wait till you see the wonderful things I brought!"

The girls relieved Mama of the baskets and chattered excitedly all the way home. "Oh, I'm so tired." Mama sank into the nearest chair and let out a sigh. "Just let me sit still for a minute."

The girls waited expectantly.

After a moment, Mama reached into one of her baskets. Out came some yardage of cotton material prettily patterned with tiny yellow flowers on a background of deep blue. She held up the cloth

26

against Szerena's slim body. "It'll make up beautifully," she said.

"Oh, Mama, it's lovely!" the girls agreed.

"There's enough material there for both of
you."

Gisella ran her hand over the shiny fabric. It
felt clean and smooth. She held it close to her face,
sniffing it. There was always such a pleasing smell
about cloth that was new.

By now, Mama was unfolding some fine white
embroidery. "See! This is what I got for your underwear." She rummaged around inside the basket.
"And here's some lace to match. For ruffles."

"Mama!" The girls clasped their hands in delight. Never had they seen such finery! "It's beautiful!"

"For once, my girls will really be dressed up on
the Passover holiday," Mama declared.

From the other basket, Mama proceeded to
take out a number of small sacks — salt, sugar, assorted spices, and a jug of kerosene for the lamps.
And that seemed to be all. She picked up the empty
baskets and went to the storage room to put them
away.

Gisella and Szerena looked at each other. Gisella whispered, "She's always brought us back a
treat before."

"Maybe she had to spend too much on all the
fancy material," Szerena whispered back.

Mama returned to the room. Was that a teasing

27

glint in her eyes? "I suppose you thought I had forgotten something," she said, smiling. From her apron pocket, she drew out two somethings, sparkling and blue, dangling them in the air.

"Beads! Blue beads!" Gisella squealed.

"Gisella!" Szerena cried. "They're even prettier than what the peddler had!"

"Thanks, Mama! Thanks!" The girls shouted and threw themselves upon her, hugging and kissing her.

"Just a minute," she protested laughingly. "There's more!"

"More?"

"My regular customer was in a very good mood today. She asked, 'How are my two girls?' Then she gave me this little present for you." From her other apron pocket, Mama pulled out a paper cone and unfolded it. Inside were two red whistles.

"Such a nice lady!" Szerena exclaimed. She put her whistle to her mouth and blew. It sounded a high clear note. Then a look of delighted surprise crossed her face. She took the whistle out, licking her lips. "It's made of candy!" she cried. "Imagine that! A candy whistle!"

"Candy?" Gisella repeated joyfully. "We haven't had any candy for ages and ages!"

Szerena's whistle was licked away very rapidly. But Gisella held on to hers. It was just the most wonderful treat! Gingerly she put the whistle to her lips and blew softly. How delicious it tasted! She bit a tiny piece off the very bottom where it wouldn't really matter. "Mmm!" She rolled the sweetness around on her tongue.

Suddenly she remembered Mama. "Want some, Mama?" she offered.

Mama smiled. "No, my darling. You enjoy it."

"I'm not going to eat mine now. I'm going to save it for tomorrow."

Szerena's whistle was all gone. But Gisella wrapped hers back in the paper and tucked it into her apron pocket. There it remained until bedtime, though every once in a while, her fingers could not resist curling themselves around it. Tomorrow, she kept promising herself.

That night it lay under her pillow. In the morning it went back into her apron pocket.

"Aren't you ever going to eat it?" Szerena asked.

"I will. Later."

However, by late afternoon, Gisella could hold out no longer. Leaning against the front gate, she took the whistle from its paper and carefully put it in her mouth. Gently she sucked, then withdrew it. She licked it some more. Took it out. I mustn't eat it too fast, she cautioned herself. It may be a long time before I get any more.

Just then she spied her friend Ilona skipping up the road. "Gisella!" Ilona shouted. "Want to come over to my house?"

Gisella started blowing away noisily on her

whistle so Ilona would notice.

"What have you got there?" Ilona asked.

"Oh, just a candy whistle," Gisella replied in an offhand manner. She knew that Ilona got candy lots of times. Her papa was rich. He had a big farm, and Ilona lived in a house with a roof made of shingles. Not of mud and earth and straw, like theirs. Maybe if her papa were here, she would get candy every day. Smiling at Ilona, she said aloud, "Want some?" She turned the whistle around and held it out to her. "Here. Bite off from this side."

The tip was wet and slippery-gooey. As Ilona bent forward to bite, the whistle slithered through Gisella's fingers and fell to the ground!

"Ooh!" gasped Gisella. She stared dumbfounded at the precious candy lying in the dust at her feet. A moment ago it was bright red. Now it looked all messy. Utter dismay pulled down the corners of her mouth. It wasn't fair! It just wasn't! She'd been waiting and waiting — and now just look what an awful thing had happened!

I could pick it up, she told herself in desperation. If I took it into the house and washed it off, it would be as good as new. But Ilona is watching. What would she think if I went and did a thing like that! I'd be too ashamed. Besides, I'm sure Ilona would never eat a piece of candy that had been in the dirt, even if it was washed off. It's no use. I just have to leave it lying there.

Oh, she thought, full of misery. If only Ilona

30

hadn't come by. Then I would still have my candy.

"Too bad!" Ilona sympathized.

Gisella forced a smile to her lips, though she felt miserable. "It doesn't matter," she said slowly, and ground the whistle to bits with her heel. "My mama will get me some more. Come on. We'll go to your house."

She forced herself to go skipping lightheartedly along with Ilona.

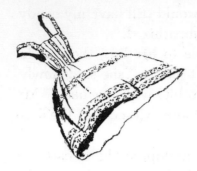

THREE

FOR MORE than a week, the kitchen in the synagogue was all hustle and bustle. Each day a different group of women, and some of the men too, had pitched in to help. Today it was for Mama's family.

"Mama, do you think we should take Gisella along?" teased Szerena. "She'll only get in the way."

"I will not!" Gisella snapped. "I can help just as much as you!"

"Well, all right then," Szerena said, smiling. "You can measure the water."

"Now let's see," Mama considered, "I'll need clean linens. And, of course, my special basket and rolling pin. They're up in the attic."

"I'll get them for you," offered Szerena.

"No, Szerena. The basket's too big for you to handle," Mama said. "You get the linen."

In the front room, Mama quickly climbed the ladder leading to the attic, her wide skirt billowing out with each step. In a moment, she had disappeared from view, but they could hear the boards creaking overhead.

"I guess we can't take the basket we always use, can we?" Gisella said.

"You know better," Szerena replied. "On Passover we're not allowed to use the same utensils we use throughout the year. That's why we have special Passover dishes. And even though we do use the same cutlery and the stove, they'll be scoured thoroughly to make sure they're kosher for the Passover."

Mama came down the ladder with the big basket bouncing before her. "Put the linen in the basket, Szerena. Then let's all hurry and wash up. The women will be waiting."

Faces and arms were scrubbed diligently. Then all three donned freshly laundered cotton dresses and clean white aprons.

"Come. Let's go," Mama said.

"But, Mama, you forgot the flour!" Gisella reminded.

"No, my child. Remember that extra-fine wheat we saved after the harvest last fall? We put

33

it away in the special linen sack that has our name on it? Well, early this morning, while you were still asleep, I carried it to the miller for grinding. Afterward I took it to the synagogue. It's in the kitchen there right now."

Gisella skipped gaily alongside Szerena. Everything about the coming holiday made things so different! "You know, Szerena, I'm glad the Jews didn't have time to wait for their bread to rise when Moses led them out of Egypt."

"Why?"

"Because then they had to eat unleavened bread. So now we have to eat it too. And I just love matzo. It's always so crisp and makes such crunchy noises when you eat it. And it's such fun making it."

"Not everyone makes their own matzo," Mama said. "In the big cities, Jewish people buy their matzo."

"Buy their matzo!" Gisella exclaimed, feeling sorry for the city people. "I wouldn't like that at all! I'm glad we live right here where we can make our own."

The matzo bakers were already assembled in the synagogue kitchen when they arrived. "I'm so glad to see you!" Zali Neni cried, enfolding the girls in her chubby arms.

In Helmecz all adult men were called *Bacsi* (Uncle) and all older women were given the title of *Neni* (Aunt). Zali Neni, however, was the chil-

34

dren's real aunt. No one could ever have guessed she was Mama's sister. Mama was usually so serious and slim and had blue eyes, while Zali Neni was jolly and fat, with plump rosy cheeks and dark eyes that always sparkled brightly. Zali Neni had only sons — three of them. She missed not having a daughter, so Mama's girls were especially dear to her. Turning to Mama, she said, "Well, Rezi, let's get to work."

Whereupon the women rolled up their sleeves and gathered around the long table.

"Bring on the flour!" cried an elderly woman.

One of the men lifted Mama's sack. Walking around the table, he shook out a small heap of flour in front of each place. Close behind him came Gisella and poured a measure of water into every heap.

Immediately the women fell to stirring and mixing till each had a lump of workable dough. Gisella watched fascinated as with skill born of many years, they began to knead, their faces shiny from the heat of the big wall oven. As they worked the dough, they laughed and gossiped with one another and joked with the men. Back and forth, back and forth, the lump rolled beneath the heel of the hand, till it lay in a smooth, roundish mound. Wielding a long knife, a man set about quickly slicing the mounds into proper sized pieces. Again each piece was kneaded, and then with swift sure strokes, the women began using their rolling pins.

35

Roll, roll, and turn the dough — roll and roll and turn — and before Gisella's admiring eyes, the pieces were transformed into a tableful of large flat circles. She saw Mama was beaming with pride, because Szerena stood working right along with the women.

"Could I have a piece of dough," she ventured, "so I could make my own matzo?"

"Why not?" laughed Zali Neni, and threw a piece of dough across to Gisella. "Here, darling, enjoy yourself."

Gisella flashed her a pleased smile. Prickles of excitement bubbled through her. In this gay, lively place, with everyone lending a hand, work became a joyous thing. Back and forth she seesawed the rolling pin the way the women did. "It feels so bouncy!" she cried, giggling.

"It's supposed to," Szerena said in her big sister manner, "otherwise you couldn't shape it."

Gisella continued with her rolling. "Why is it coming out so funny?" she complained after a while. "It's not round like everybody else's."

She frowned. It had seemed so easy when she had watched the others. But just look at her piece. First one corner stuck way out, then another. She rolled and stretched — rip — she had stretched it too much. The dough tore! There was a big hole right in the middle! "Ooh!" Gisella wailed.

Zali Neni burst into laughter. "Oh, Gisella, now you can wear it around your neck!"

Everyone laughed, even Gisella.

"Try again and I'll help you," Mama said, giving her a fresh piece of dough. She placed her hand over Gisella's and guided the rolling pin. Presto! There was another smooth round circle ready for baking.

Presently, down the length of the table went the man with the pricking wheel. Skillfully he kept running it across the flat circles, making even rows of needle holes.

"The tiny holes let the air escape while the matzos are baking," Mama explained to Gisella. "That way they won't curl up or break."

"And it makes a pretty design," Szerena added. "Especially after it's baked."

"Ready for the baking!" the women called out.

Immediately the helper brought over an especially long, flat wooden paddle. Scooping two of the dough circles from the table, he draped them over the paddle and carried them to the oven. Gisella trailed after him.

"One of those matzos is mine," she informed him. "I have to watch it so it won't get mixed up with the others."

The helper smiled. "Don't worry, Gisella. I'll put a mark on it with my wheel. Then we'll know positively it's your property."

At the oven, the shoveler took over. Placing Gisella's circle on his long-handled wooden paddle, he slid it into the oven on a bed of hot ashes. In no time at all, it turned into a firm, crisp, brown-flecked matzo with a big "G" dotting its white surface.

Gisella was delighted. "My own matzo! It came out just perfect!"

By this time, a second paddle was on its way over the ashes. One after the other, the shoveler kept feeding the dough into the hot mouth of the oven.

On the floor, near the stove, fresh straw was already spread. Mama had covered it with one of her large tablecloths. As each matzo was baked, the shoveler gently deposited it on the tablecloth. Bits of gray-black ash still clung to the cooling matzo. An elderly man stood by and carefully brushed the ash away with a large goose-wing brush.

Mama placed another tablecloth inside her basket, and she and the elderly brusher began stacking the matzos. Gisella counted out loud as each matzo was tucked into place. There were just two hundred of them, filling the basket to overflowing. Gisella's initialed matzo was placed right on top.

"Mama, so many matzos!" Gisella exclaimed.

"We'll need plenty. Don't forget Passover lasts for eight days. And if there are any left over, we can still eat them."

It was time for cleaning up. The table was cleared, and the utensils washed. The fire in the oven was banked. Tomorrow Mama would be helping some other family bake their matzos.

Szerena helped Mama carry the basket home. Mama wrapped a second cloth around it and bound it securely with rope. This was to make sure that no trace of *hometz* (non-Passover things) would touch it.

The next day, after school, Mama and the girls went to Anna Neni's house for the final fitting of their new clothes. Anna Neni, the village dressmaker, owned a sewing machine. She was very proud of it. No one else in the whole village had a sewing machine.

Gisella and Szerena never ceased to marvel at the way it worked. They watched, fascinated, as Anna Neni's feet pedaled swiftly, while her hands guided the material past the dancing needle. "It's so fast, you can't see how it's done!" Szerena cried. "A million times faster than sewing by hand!"

"Look at the tiny, even stitches it makes!" Gisella added. "Not zigzaggy like mine." She sidled up to Szerena. "Wouldn't you just love to try it?" she whispered in her ear.

"Yes," Szerena whispered back. "But she won't let us. She never allows anyone to even touch it. A machine like that must cost an awful lot of money."

"I wish we had a sewing machine," Gisella said, sighing.

"Maybe when we're in America, Papa will buy

us one," Szerena said, her eyes lighting up at the thought.

Gisella had a sudden feeling of uneasiness. That's no reason for going all the way to America, she thought. She shook off thinking about it. Nothing had been settled yet. We're still right here in Helmecz.

Anna Neni pushed her chair away from the machine and stood up. She was middle-aged and thin; her shoulders were stooped from long hours spent bending over her sewing. Silently, she helped the girls into their dresses and examined her work with a critical eye.

She hardly ever talks, Gisella thought. Maybe that's because she always has pins in her mouth.

"Hmm." Anna Neni finally grunted, with a little nod of her head. She turned her gaze upon Mama, awaiting her verdict.

"Beautiful, Anna! Just beautiful!" Mama enthused. "They fit so well! Tomorrow the girls will bring you a bushel of potatoes and a dozen fresh eggs in payment. You've done a fine job!"

Anna Neni lifted her shoulders slightly as if to say, "It's nothing," but a faint smile fluttered on her lips. "Wear them in good health," she mumbled to the girls.

Gisella nudged Szerena. "Anna Neni," Szerena spoke up, "is there any material left over?"

The dressmaker nodded. "Yes. I saved the scraps for you." She rummaged through her bag.

"Here you are."

"They're for my sister's doll," Szerena said. "We're going to make her some new clothes."

Gisella hugged the small pieces of cloth to her. "My doll must be dressed up for Passover, too."

At home, Mama laid the clothes away in the shiny black chest. "Till Thursday," she said, shutting the lid.

Often during the next few days, the girls raised the lid to catch yet another glimpse of their new clothes. "I can hardly wait till Thursday!" Gisella kept repeating.

It was the afternoon of the day before Passover. Mama and Szerena were working in the vegetable garden. Gisella had sneaked into the house, and once again she knelt before the chest and looked rapturously at the outfits Anna Neni had made.

How pretty they were! Lovingly she fingered the rows of tiny tucks, the puffed sleeves, the little underpants with their lace ruffles. The petticoats were beautiful with their delicate eyelet-embroidery insertions and straps made of dainty lace. Never in her life had she had anything so exquisite!

Tenderly she lifted the petticoat and held it up to her. What a shame to hide such a beautiful petticoat under a dress! Before she knew it, Gisella had shed her pinafore, dress, and her petticoat. The next minute found her in her brand new petticoat. Holding the skirt out, she danced around

41

and around the room and out the door.

The late April air had a touch of chill, but Gisella didn't notice. Proudly she paraded up and down the road.

Old Mr. Czatordoy came strolling by. He grinned broadly at her as he passed, and Gisella was very pleased. Oh, she told herself, he likes my petticoat. Others who came along seemed equally entertained. Some even laughed.

All at once, Gisella heard Mama call. "Gisella! Come into the house this very instant!"

Before she even had time to obey, Mama was already outside, grasping her by the arm and steering her toward the door. "How could you!" she scolded.

"But, Mama ——"

Mama wouldn't listen. Quickly she pushed Gisella into the house. "What's gotten into you?" she gasped as soon as the door shut behind them. "Standing around in the street like that where everybody can see you!"

Gisella couldn't understand why Mama was making such a fuss. "But, Mama," she pleaded, puzzled, "everybody admired my petticoat. It's so beautiful!"

"Oh, Gisella!" Mama's mouth was puckered up with displeasure. "Before all the neighbors in your underwear! What will they think?"

Szerena laughed. "Maybe people thought it was a new style."

FOUR

PASSOVER starts tonight, and there is still so much to do," Mama declared in gay complaint. "It's lucky that this year Easter and our Passover holiday come at the same time."

"Why?" asked Gisella.

"Because with the school closed, you're both here to help me."

"What shall we do next?" Szerena inquired.

"Strip the beds," Mama replied.

When this was done, Mama refilled the bottoms with sweet-smelling fresh straw from the barn. Over the straw, the girls spread handwoven linen sheets. Pillows were plumped into place on top of the full, down quilts, and the freshly-laundered red

43

spreads were smoothed over the top of everything.

Earthen floors were swept, windows cleaned, furniture polished. The Passover dishes were set out in the front room, on the shelves on either side of the big wall oven. Underneath the shelves, they hung the pots and pans scoured to mirrorlike brightness. So much water was used up in the scrubbing and cleaning that the rain barrel was nearly empty.

In between, Mama managed to attend to her cooking. In the big room, all kinds of delicious things were bubbling and boiling on top of the square black cookstove. A special Passover cake was slowly baking in the oven. Such heavenly smells filled the air!

Mama cast a glance at the nearly empty wood pails beside the stove. "Szerena, better bring in some more wood," she said. She looked down. "We swept the floors, but we haven't wet them down yet."

"I'll do that! Let me do that!" Gisella begged.

"All right," Mama nodded indulgently.

Gisella skipped off to the storage room for the watering can which she filled with the last remaining water in the rain barrel.

As she sprinkled, the ground upon which she stood no longer seemed an earthen floor. It became like an enormous sheet of drawing paper. Slowly she moved from one corner to another dribbling the water up and down, crisscross, and round about. What fun to see the ribbonlike designs taking shape!

44

The moist patterns stood out sharply. But alas, not for long. The greedy earth sucked in the water, and the outlines paled and vanished. Once again the ground, now hardened and smooth, was just dark brown earth.

By this time, Mama had two plump chickens prepared in the roasting pan ready to pop into the stove. "It's a little early yet," she remarked. "I guess I'll roast them this afternoon."

"Two chickens, Mama?" exclaimed Gisella.

"Don't forget about our guests, Estzer Neni and her little daughter Juli. And old Bela Bacsi who will conduct the Seder for us, and you know how much he can eat." She laughed, but the laughter turned into a sigh. "Please God the day will come when Papa will sit at the head of our table and conduct the Passover service."

Gisella tried to imagine a Seder table with a papa reclining in the big chair, with pillows behind his back, like a king. And Mama as his queen. That would be nice she had to admit.

"That reminds me," Mama broke in. She went to the chest, took out their holiday clothes, and laid them out neatly on one of the beds.

Gisella jumped up. "Can we put them on now?"

"Not yet," Mama said. "Right now I'm going over to the widow Salomon's to see if there is something I can do for her. I heard she is not feeling well." She poured some soup into a jar and took a large piece of the still-warm cake. "I won't be too long. But remember," she held up a warning finger, "I don't want either of you to leave the house. A band of Gypsies is in our neighborhood this week. They're camped out in the meadow at the foot of the hills. So don't you go wandering off by yourselves, you hear?"

"We won't, Mama," the girls promised. They seated themselves on the porchlike shelf outside and watched Mama going off. After a while, they got up and strolled in the little garden following the path of a whistling bird.

"Wouldn't you like to go over to Mari's house and see her new doll?" suggested Gisella. "All the other girls have seen it already. They say it's just marvelous!"

"I know. Her mother got it from those rich people she works for in the city," Szerena said. "I would like to see it."

"Well — let's go," Gisella promptly decided.

"Mama said not to leave the house."

"But it's just across the street. We don't have to stay long. We'll just take a quick look and run right back."

Szerena hesitated. "I don't think we ought to."

"Oh, come on," urged Gisella. "We'll come right back."

"All right." Szerena gave in.

Hand in hand they dashed across the street and into Mari's house.

Mari was ten years old. Gisella thought she was very pretty. She had long brown hair hanging down her back, and rosy cheeks, and wide-open blue eyes. "I guess you've come to see my doll," she gloated. "Right now she's sleeping there on my bed. I'll get her."

She lifted the doll and held it in her arms.

"Oh!" Gisella breathed. "How beautiful!"

They gaped with awe at the doll. She was more than a foot long and dressed in red calico sprigged with tiny blue flowers. She wore a stiff, white organdy petticoat and cunning little shoes on her feet.

"See! She has real hair," Mari said boastfully, stroking the doll's curly brown locks. "Watch!" She tipped the doll's head gently backward and forward. "She opens and shuts her eyes! Just like a real baby!"

"I never dreamed they could make dolls like that!" Szerena cried. "Look, Gisella," she put out her hand, "her face is like porcelain."

Mari backed away. "You mustn't touch!" Her arms tightened possessively. "I can't allow anyone to touch her. She's much too precious."

She held the doll up tantalizingly high, laughing up at it. "Oh, I just love her!" she cried. Then she cradled it in her arms and swayed as if rocking it to sleep.

Gisella's heart was filled with immense yearning. If she could only hold the doll for just one

moment! Her arms reached out. "Mari, please —
could I. . .?"

"No!" Mari swung away from her, holding the
doll out of reach. "She's too delicate. She could
easily break."

"But I'll be so very careful," Gisella pleaded.
Mari shook her head.

"Well, then, can I at least touch her?"

"No!" Mari repeated stubbornly. "I'm sorry.
But you can come over and look at her whenever
you like." She sat down with the doll in her lap
and began fussing with it. She spread its dainty
skirt and caused the eyes to open and close. "My
doll is getting sleepy," she said. "I have to put her
to bed."

Szerena tugged at Gisella's sleeve. "Come," she
coaxed, "we've got to get back."

Gisella found it hard to tear herself away.
"Just another minute," she begged.

"Mama's bound to come home soon. She'll be
angry if she finds we're not there."

One last wistful, lingering glance, and Gisella
permitted herself to be led away. As they crossed
the street, she muttered. "I only wanted to touch it.
She could have let me touch it. If I had a doll like
that, I'd let all my friends touch it. I'd even let
them play with it."

Szerena felt sorry for her little sister. "I don't
mind for myself," she said. "After all, I'm already
too grown-up for dolls. I was just anxious to see it.

I've never known anyone who had such a doll. But not letting you play with it, that's really mean. She's mean and selfish, that Mari. That's what she is!" She gave Gisella's hand a little squeeze. "Never mind. Just don't think about it."

But Gisella couldn't be consoled. Never would she forget that lovely doll. She vowed to Szerena, "Someday when I grow up and marry and have a little girl of my own, I'm going to buy her a doll just like that, no matter how much it costs!"

The door of the house was wide open. "You left the door open!" Szerena cried.

"But I didn't!" protested Gisella.

They poked their heads inside. "Oh!" Gisella shrieked, clapping her hands to her head. "The whole barnyard's in there!"

Chickens were everywhere, scratching and clucking away contentedly as they wandered through the house. Two roosters were leaping at each other, fighting for possession of the bed. A goose had managed to get onto the table and was greedily pecking away at the remains of Mama's Passover cake. Several others were floundering about in the open chest. Even their one turkey gobbler was resting in solitary majesty on top of a wood pail. Immediately the girls scooted about, shouting at the top of their lungs, "Shoo! Shoo! Out! Out of here! Out!"

The bewildered fowl, squawking and cackling, went flying every which way trying to escape. For a few deafening moments, all was pandemonium. But finally the house was cleared of feathered folk, and the door slammed shut. The girls, out of breath, flopped down onto the wooden chest.

Ruefully they surveyed the room. "What a mess!" Gisella wailed. "After all our hard work this morning, too."

All at once both of them stared at the beds. One of them was lacking its red spread! And where were their new clothes?

Gisella gripped Szerena's arm. "Oh, Szerena! The chest is open!" Her face blanched. She dared not voice what she was thinking.

Szerena felt a flutter of fear cross her stomach. Where was Mama?

In a panic, they made for the door. But before they could reach it, it was flung open, and they were caught up in Mama's arms. She held them very tight. "Thank God!" she sobbed. "Thank God . . . you're all right!" The words seemed to tear out in gasps. "I was so afraid. Oh — thank God!"

Shaken by Mama's frantic manner, the girls clung to her, whimpering, "Mama, Mama!"

How strange and disheveled Mama appeared! Her kerchief was gone; her hair straggly over her anguished face. Her white blouse was stained a dirty brown and had pulled loose from her skirt belt. Through a tear on one side of her skirt, they could see a blood stain. "Mama," they screamed, "you're hurt!"

Gently they helped her to a chair. She winced a little as she sat down. Gisella knelt beside her, stroking her hand. Szerena hurriedly wet a cloth and pressed it to the cut on Mama's leg.

"Thank you, my sweet children," Mama murmured, smiling wanly. "Shush now — shush," she tried to reassure them. "It's all right — all right."

Her eyes traveled around the room. She gave a deep sigh, then said, "We've been robbed."

"We didn't know what had happened," Szerena whispered, bursting into tears.

Mama's head moved sadly up and down. "All my best linen and tablecloths — the red bedspread — and heaven knows what else!"

"Our clothes, too?" Gisella broke in, knowing the answer, yet hoping against hope.

Mama's face was gray with fatigue. "Yes, my darlings, I'm afraid your new clothes, too."

"Oh!" Gisella sank into a dejected little heap on the floor. All their beautiful holiday clothes gone! IIow could anyone be so horrible as to steal them!

"I see even the pot with the chickens I prepared for roasting was stolen," Mama went on sorrowfully. She stroked Gisella's blond head. "Shush. Shush, my children. Don't cry anymore. Just think how much worse it could have been. You might have been harmed in some way. I might — God forbid — have lost you both!" She drew them close. Thus they clung together for a long time till the

51

tears had ceased to flow. Then Mama began to tell what had happened.

"When I came back to the house and found the door wide open, I knew immediately something was wrong. I rushed inside, and when I saw all this, my first thought was that you had been kidnapped! But then I asked myself, when could it have happened? I had been away such a short time. And you were both here up to the moment I'd gone. Whoever had made off with you, couldn't be far away. I felt sure it was the Gypsies, and I figured they wouldn't dare take the main road for fear of being seen. So I ran to the back of the house, and there I saw large footprints in the soft earth. I realized then that the thief must be heading across the open fields.

"I ran and ran. My heart was beating like a hammer. Then I saw him — a tall, thin man walking rapidly, with a pack on his back. I knew I had found the thief, because the pack was my good red bedspread all bulged out with the things he'd stolen.

"I yelled for help. But there was no one around to hear me. So I began to run even faster till I caught up with the thief. I grabbed hold of his arm and screamed at him. 'What have you done with my children?' "

Gisella shivered. "Oh, Mama! Weren't you afraid?"

"I had no time to think about being afraid."

She brushed a lock of hair from her forehead. "He tried to shake me off, but I hung on for dear life. 'Kidnapper! Thief!' I kept yelling. 'Where are my children?' I remember I beat at him with my fists.

" 'Get away from me! I know nothing about your children!' he shouted. He turned and glared at me." Mama put a hand to her chest. "I'll remember that evil face till the day I die! He snarled at me, and then he hit me across the face. But still I wouldn't let go. He kept pressing on ahead, dragging me along with him.

"He struck at me again and again. I fell. I can't remember very clearly what happened after that. I must have fainted. Anyway, when I came to, the road was empty. The thief had disappeared, up toward the hills, I suppose. There was nothing more I could do except to run to the magistrate and our neighbors for help. But first I had to come home and take another look. So I came running back, praying all the while that I'd find you here." She covered her eyes with her hands and sat very still.

"Mama," Szerena whispered, "your leg. It's still bleeding. Maybe we should get the doctor."

Mama examined the wound. "It must have been cut when I was being dragged along. It's not too bad. I can take care of it myself." She rose, limped over to the attic ladder and slowly climbed up, with Gisella and Szerena helping her along.

In a corner of the attic, Mama searched around till she found a large spider web. With the utmost care, she loosened it from its fastenings and spread it across the wound. The silvery, sticky threads adhered instantly to the cuts. "This will heal it nicely. In a few days, my leg will be as good as new. By the way," Mama asked suddenly, "where were you both when the thief was in the house?"

"Across the street in Mari's house," Szerena replied, shamefaced. "We wanted to see her new doll. We intended to come right back. . . ."

"Well, for this once I cannot be angry with you for disobeying me. The angel Elijah himself must have sent you there. Otherwise . . ." her shoulders hunched, and she clasped her hands together tightly ". . . better not even to think about it."

Soon they were back downstairs. Mama told the girls, "I must go at once to see the *biro* to report the robbery. Just look at this mess! Tsk!" she clicked dolefully. "All topsy-turvy! Well, we'll have to take care of it later. Right now I have to make myself presentable."

By the time she had washed, combed her hair, and donned a fresh skirt and blouse, Mama was her calm self again. "Come," she said, "we'll lock up the house, and I'll drop you both off at Zali Neni's. You'll stay with her till I get back."

News of the robbery fanned through the village like a forest fire. Upon Mama's return, neighbors came flocking to the house bearing gifts of food and linen to replace what had been stolen. "Poor Rezi Neni. Such a calamity!" they kept exclaiming, with much head shaking and gesturing. "And to have it happen on the very eve of Passover, too!"

"What did the *biro* say?" someone inquired.

"He was very sympathetic," Mama replied. "But he explained that he was only the *biro,* and this was a task for the *csendor.* And we don't have a policeman in Helmecz."

"There is a *csendor* in the village of Laz," offered a woman.

"That's not very far," put in another.

Mama nodded. "I know. The *biro* has already gone to Laz to fetch him. They should be here shortly."

Within the hour, the *biro* and *csendor* were in the house. Gisella and Szerena had never before seen a policeman. They could not take their eyes off him. How resplendent he looked in his brass-buttoned blue uniform, topped by a visored hat from which a plume of brightly colored feathers stood up gaily! He was very tall, and the red stripe running down the side of each trouser leg made him appear even taller. He spoke with authority but was most polite, bending forward courteously to listen to Mama.

"Every time those roving bands of Gypsies appear, there's bound to be trouble," he commented, frowning.

The neighbors nodded in silent agreement.

"But we will see what can be done," he went on. "I know they've set up their camp in the hills, but they like to do their trading in Ungwar. It's too late to go there now. But they'll be lined up in the marketplace tomorrow morning. They'll have their merchandise spread out on the ground. I dare say much of what they offer for sale is stolen. But we can't always prove it. You know your own things. If they have them, you're bound to recognize them." He bowed ceremoniously. "I'll call for you in the morning. Good day to you all."

Mama slumped wearily in her chair. Zali Neni put her hand on Mama's shoulder. "You've had a terrible day. Go lie down for a while. The girls will help me straighten up here."

"That's right. And don't worry," the neighbors chimed in. "If there's anything you want, you need only ask."

"As for the Seder," Jozsi Bacsi announced, "nothing's lost. Zali and I want you and the children and your guests to come to ours. You'll all be guests at our Seder."

Mama looked around with gratitude. "It's good to have family and friends in time of trouble," she said, her voice trembling.

Szerena marched proudly alongside the *csendor*. Gisella held tight to Mama's hand, but all the while the edge of her eyes noted everything. The Gypsies and their wares were already settled at one end of the square. They appeared ragged and unkempt and yet strangely attractive. The men, slen-

56

der and dark-haired, wore brightly hued shirts and golden loops in their ears. The women, in gay, swirling skirts, moved with an easy grace, lifting their heads pridefully. As they wheedled and harangued the passersby, arms and hands danced, white teeth flashed from swarthy faces. Even the small children cavorting about stared back impudently at her.

Slowly they made their way down the length of the street. Mama searched through the assorted merchandise and scanned every male face. As the *csendor* passed by, one young Gypsy laughed and said mockingly to his mate, "High and mighty is the peacock! Always coming around to cackle!"

There was sudden quiet among the spectators. They glanced furtively at the *csendor*. His countenance remained unmoved, but with a sudden motion, he raised his hand and struck the Gypsy across the mouth.

Gisella winced almost as if her mouth had been slapped. Still — how dare he talk like that to a *csendor!*

The Gypsy seemed cowed. But his burning eyes were alive with hate. The whole Gypsy market ceased its chattering. Gisella could feel the smouldering tenseness in the air. Mama turned to the *csendor*. "I'm afraid my things are not here. Neither is the thief."

Scornful, triumphant glances darted from one Gypsy face to another. But the *csendor* was not yet

57

finished with them. "The thief's probably been warned," he said. "Who knows how far away he may be by now. Well, there's nothing more I can do except make sure that it won't happen again." In a loud and commanding voice, he said, "All you Gypsies, pack up your things and get out immediately! Every one of you! If there is a single one left in this district by tomorrow morning, I'll have him locked up!"

He turned to Mama. "I'm very sorry about your things."

"You did everything you could," Mama assured him. "I thank you." She sighed. "This will be a Passover we will long remember."

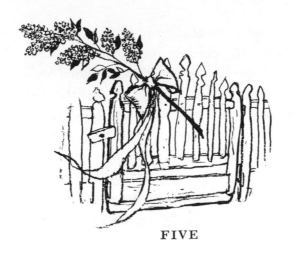

FIVE

My dearest Wife,

I was so glad to hear from you and to learn that you are all well. I cannot tell you how proud it makes me to see how beautifully our little Szerena writes. And Gisella's words, too. It's hard to realize that they are old enough to do this for you. In my mind I still see them as little babies.

And now for a piece of wonderful news! I now have my own business!

The job at the cigar factory was not bad. But working like this, it would take, God knows how long, before I'd be able to put by enough money to bring over my family. The *only way, I decided, was to own my own business — be my own boss. Now I am able to speak English quite well. So I started looking around, and by luck I found just the right place — a small fruit and vegetable stand. It is tiring work and a long day. I have to get up at three o'clock in the morning to get to the wholesale market to buy the produce. Then back to my little place where I stay till late at night waiting on the customers. But I do not mind. It is for our future — yours and mine.*

Of course, every penny I saved had to go into the business. But business is very good. I am making money. I figure that in a year I shall have it all paid for and enough left over to send for you. By then I shall be a full citizen, too. I just need my second papers. My first I have already.

I know you will be needing some money for the Passover holiday. So I send you a money order for $10.00 and also a present for each of the girls.

My heartfelt love to all of you.
Herschel

"It's like money from heaven, even if it is too late for Passover," declared Mama. "What with the robbery, it couldn't have come at a better time."

As for the girls, they were overwhelmed with

60

delight. Papa had sent identical dresses in green and red cotton plaid with hair ribbons to match.

"Isn't the pattern odd!" Szerena exclaimed. "We don't have material with stripes like this."

Picking up her new dress, Gisella walked over to the window. The late afternoon sunshine cast a sheen of gold over the brightly patterned cloth. It's like a miracle, she mused. Almost as if Papa knew our holiday clothes had been stolen. But how could that be? He couldn't possibly have gotten our letter yet.

"Papa's always so generous and kind," she heard Mama say. "He never forgets us."

A jumble of feelings tore at Gisella. She wanted to be angry at a papa who had gone away and left them! But — her eyes lowered to the dress in her arms — it was beautiful!

"Lucky for us the package didn't get here before Passover," Mama went on, "otherwise the thief would have stolen these dresses, too."

"Well, they didn't get here in time for Passover," Szerena chimed in, "but they're just in time for *Majus Nap*."

"That's right," Mama responded cheerfully. "But that's tomorrow. Let's put them away in the chest now."

"May day! Wonderful, joyous *Majus Nap!*" chanted Gisella. She waltzed lightheartedly out of the door and around the back of the house. She came to a halt before the woodpile where Imre, their neighbor's son, was neatly stacking the wood he'd cut for Mama.

"Imre, have you fixed up your branch yet?" she asked.

"Branch?" he repeated in his quiet voice. "What branch?"

"For tomorrow. Tomorrow is *Majus Nap*."

"So?"

"So you have to fix up a branch. One with blossoms on it. Or even just plain leaves from a tree."

"And then?"

"Then you must make it look even prettier with ribbons and bows."

"So then what happens?"

"So then, in the middle of the night when everybody is fast asleep, you creep out and stick it either on the gate or the fence of the house of the girl you love."

Imre continued piling the wood. "Oh, you mean *that* silly custom."

"It is not silly!" Gisella protested. "I think it's a lovely idea!"

Under his thatch of sandy-colored hair, Imre's blue eyes beamed down on her with amusement. "You really think so?"

"Oh, Imre! You know you're just teasing." They both exploded into laughter.

"I guess that whole business must seem romantic to a girl," Imre admitted. "But I don't notice any of the Jewish lads doing it."

"No. I don't know why."

Imre shrugged. "Different people, different customs, I guess. There are many interesting celebrations the Jews observe that we Christians don't."

"Imre, who's your girl?"

Imre pretented to think hard. "Oh, she's little and has green eyes. Her hair is like white gold. And she always wears it in braids."

"Who can that be?" inquired Gisella.

Imre poked his finger at her. "Why, you, of course."

"Oh, Imre!" Gisella giggled. "You're teasing again. Can I see your branch when you've fixed it up?"

"Who knows? Maybe I'll get my girl to show it to you tomorrow."

Gisella danced back into the house. "He's so nice, that Imre," she announced. "And he's always doing all those things for us."

"He gets paid for it," Szerena reminded.

"He doesn't get very much," remarked Mama. "And many's the time he has refused to take anything. Yes, he really is a very fine young man."

Next morning Gisella woke to the first crow of the cock. Bounding out of bed, she flew to the window. Pinkish clouds, like a fleet of ships, were sailing across the green-streaked sky. The rising sun was just barely winking at her. "Szerena, wake up!" Gisella cried. "It's a beautiful day!"

Mama didn't have to coax them to hurry with

their chores today. As soon as they were through, they hastened to dress for the school outing. Brown sandals, ribbons in perky bows on their heads, and finally the new plaid frocks.

Mama packed their lunch in a neat cloth bundle and gave them each two fillers to spend.

"Two pennies!" cried Szerena.

"Ooh! So much money! Oh, Mama, thanks!" they chorused.

"From Papa," she told them, smiling into their upturned faces.

They gave her a hug and kiss and started off.

"Have a good time," she called after them.

Holding hands, they ran quickly down the path toward the street. "Oh!" Gisella grasped her sister's arm. She pointed to the long lilac branch fastened to their gate. It was covered with clusters of delicate lavender blossoms through which a yellow satin ribbon was entwined. And where the blossoms ended, the shiny ribbon was looped in a big bow with long floating streamers.

"Who do you suppose put it there?" Szerena exclaimed.

"Imre!" Gisella responded at once.

Szerena giggled. "It would be just like him to play such a trick."

Gisella buried her face in the sweet blossoms. "It's so lovely!"

"Yes, it is," admitted Szerena. "I must say he did go to a lot of trouble just for us."

For us? Gisella repeated silently. She knew in her heart that Imre had really meant that branch for her. "Yes," she agreed, "he certainly did."

"Let's take it along," proposed Szerena. "Then we can show it off to everybody."

"Oh, no!" Gisella said quickly. "It'll get spoiled. And the ribbons will be all crushed, too. Why don't we leave it right here? It looks so pretty where it is. And then we can be sure to see it when we come home."

By the time they arrived, most of the children were already assembled at the foot of the steep path leading up to the schoolhouse.

"Say," Ilona greeted, "where'd you get those pretty striped dresses?"

"From America!" Szerena replied happily. "My papa sent them."

The girls all gathered around to ooh and aah over the wonderful frocks. It made the sisters feel very proud.

"Let's get our branches while we're waiting," suggested one of the older boys.

"Yes. Let's!" Everyone scampered across the road to the tall trees at the edge of the forest. Carefully the older boys began snapping off the smaller branches. By the time their teacher arrived, each child was supplied with a leafy branch.

Swiftly they formed themselves into two lines, as they always did when coming home from school. Only today, they were not quite so orderly. They pranced along behind their teacher, branches waving in the air like a sea of green lace. They chatted gaily, laughter rippling up and down the lines. Occasionally they burst into song. Their teacher, too, had cast off his customary stern manner. He marched ahead jauntily, his pale face wearing a broad grin.

Soon they entered a wide clearing in the forest where each year the *Majus Nap* outing was held. From all the surrounding villages, other teachers and children were pouring in to take part in the festivities. The air rang with a babble of Hungarian and Slovak.

No sooner had the Helmecz children settled themselves in a grove of trees, when it was announced that the athletic games would start.

"Let's take our shoes off. We'll be able to run faster," a boy proposed, and in a twinkling, hundreds of bare toes were enjoying the feel of the soft earth.

First there were relay races. Then followed pass-the-stick contests, jumping competitions, and the like. And all the while, youngsters stood by, bouncing up and down excitedly and screaming themselves hoarse.

When the games were over, almost everyone sprawled on the ground to relax. Some of the girls gathered leaves and wild flowers which they wove into garlands for their hair and necklaces and bracelets to match. They looked for all the world like wood nymphs come to life.

Now several fiddlers began to play a merry tune. Each school had a group ready to perform a dance which it had practiced especially for the occasion. It might be a polka, a baseda, or a czardas, or another kind of lively dance. As Gisella twirled to the spirited, stomping music of a czardas with her school friends, she was so exhilarated, she felt sure she could go on dancing forever. Especially when she remembered that this *Majus Nap* outing meant the school year was almost over.

By lunchtime, however, she was quite ready to stop. Out in the open, surrounded by one's friends, everything seemed to taste more delicious. Gisella and Szerena happily gobbled up every last morsel of the roast chicken, black bread, and sweet dried prunes Mama had packed. Afterward they helped themselves to cool water from a nearby spring.

Tradesmen from the city had set up small stands, temptingly displaying their wares. As soon as the lunch period was over, their teacher said, "I know you're all just itching to use up your spending money. So I now give permission."

Instantly, the youngsters charged toward the stands, each clamoring to purchase his share of the long awaited treats.

Gisella and Szerena elbowed their way through the milling crowd. For a while, they watched one of the candy hawkers. With a little hammer, he was breaking off appetizing chunks from an enormous slab of deep, dark chocolate. "Let's not get any of that," decided Szerena. "It melts away too fast."

Next they surveyed the candy bars. Sweets of every imaginable size, shape, and color! Gisella pointed to some puffy oblong pieces. "Look, Szerena, he's got satin pillows. Such pretty pastel shades! He's even got some that are striped!"

"They are good," Szerena agreed. "But you can get awfully tired of them. I like those tiny cherry drops. They're nice and tart. But then they're so ordinary. The candy man over there has candy whistles," she went on. "Like the ones Mama got. He has yellow ones as well as red ones. How about those?"

Gisella shook her head.

They moved on to a counter piled high with real metal whistles and rubber balls. "Who wants those?" Szerena scoffed. "We can cut our own whistles from reeds and make balls out of string. It's just a waste of money."

Then they came to a jewelry stand. Wistfully they fingered the pretty colored beads, the fancy pins, the golden bracelets, the rings with tiny stones that caught the light. Szerena frowned. "Too expensive. Anyway," she added, to console herself as well as her sister, "my friend Magda bought one of those bracelets last year, and every time she wore it, her wrist turned black. It's not real gold."

Now they considered the fancy tarts and cakes. Their eyes feasted especially on the gingerbread cookies. Should they buy the gingerbread with the picture of a little girl or boy pasted on? Or the gingerbread rabbit, or maybe a duck, or a horse? "And look at the darling little lamb," Gisella cried.

Szerena suddenly made up her mind. "I'm getting the gingerbread heart with the mirror in the center!" The next moment, she was biting off tiny bits along its edge. "Mmm! Is this good! And when I eat it all up, I'll still have a mirror. Why don't you get one?"

Gisella was tempted. She could almost taste its spicy goodness in her own mouth. But she held out. "No," she said firmly, "it has to be something extra special."

She went from stand to stand, and then something did catch her eye. A tiny porcelain doll just about three inches high. It was the prettiest thing! Until now, the only doll she'd ever owned was the one she had made herself. It had a head fashioned from clay taken from the riverbank and two crossed sticks of wood covered with cloth for the body. But this was a real doll! It had arms and legs that could move! What fun it would be sewing clothes for a real doll! Oh, if only it didn't cost too much! "How much for the doll?" she asked.

"Two fillers," the peddler said.

Gisella sighed happily. "I'll take it."

"It is darling," Szerena agreed, observing Gisella's shining face. "Here," she offered her the gingerbread, "take a bite."

69

SIX

ON THE next Sunday afternoon, Szerena
and Gisella stood at the edge of the main road
watching the wagonloads of merrymakers rolling
into Helmecz from nearby villages. The horses
trotted by on their way to the trading barn.

"The dancing will be starting soon," Szerena
said anxiously.

"Then let's run back to the house and ask
Mama if we can go," Gisella told her.

Mama was hesitant. "I don't know if you
should. You know you won't find any Jews there.
Only our Gentile neighbors."

"That doesn't matter," insisted Gisella. "They
don't mind our being there. Nobody said anything

70

when we came to watch last time."

Mama shrugged. "Oh, all right. But see that you behave yourselves. Don't get in anybody's way."

"We'll behave," the girls promised and sped quickly away.

The barn was filling up rapidly, but they found a place among the old folks and children sitting on the long benches lining the walls. Gisella looked around, her face reflecting her wonder and delight. Lamps strung from ceiling beams and set in window ledges, spread their flickering light on the rainbow colors of the decorations. It was hard to believe this was the place where peasants traded their livestock and produce during the week.

Each new group entering set up admiring huzzahs. How dazzling the young people looked in their native dress! The girls of each village vied with one another in the splendor of their outfits. Each was different and beautiful.

The girls wore dresses made of creamy white linen which they had woven. The full sleeves were hand-embroidered with elaborate original designs in a variety of brilliant colors. Over the blouse, a bright colored bodice fitted snugly, emphasizing the wearer's slender waist. Skirts were also of white linen with hemlines embroidered to match. The hand-set pleats were so narrow and so close together, the skirts fanned as wide as accordions with every turn, revealing layers of stiffly starched petticoats. A half-apron of shiny satin partially covered the skirt and was tied in back with a bewitching bow. Here and there a girl was the proud possessor of red leather boots. Some wore exquisite headdresses, crowns of satin with short multi-colored streamers dangling from either side.

"Did you ever see anything so lovely?" Gisella declared.

Szerena nodded. "It's no wonder. They've been working on their outfits for months and months. And look at the men!"

The young men looked handsome, indeed. They wore white linen trousers with elaborate embroidery along the sides and shiny black boots that came to the knee. Shirts of the same white linen were loose-sleeved and ruffled and embroidered on the front and sleeves. Their jackets were embroidered in gold and were thrown casually over one shoulder, giving them a debonair air. High-crowned hats with upturned brims completed their costumes. Some of the men had added another gay touch by putting a flower or bright feather in their hatbands.

Szerena nudged Gisella. "You notice there are no Czechs here."

"Why?"

"Because they're not invited. You know the Hungarians and the Czechs don't get along. There'd only be fights and trouble."

A small frown puckered Gisella's brow. "But

we get together with the Czech children sometimes — like on our first of May celebration."

"The teachers are made to bring them together," Szerena replied. "Maybe the Czech government thinks that's one way they'll grow up being friends instead of enemies."

Now a Gypsy band began tuning up its fiddles and zithers. Young men led their partners out on the floor. In a cascade of colors, the couples began whirling by, the girls' skirts spreading out like open parasols.

The music quickened. A czardas! Boots clicked in the air, stomped on the ground, heels dug into the earthen floor! How could anyone be expected to sit still? Children sprang from their seats and began jumping about. Szerena caught hold of Gisella and pulled her to her feet. Together they hopped and skipped and twirled.

"There's Imre!" Szerena cried. "Doesn't he look handsome!"

There was a pause in the music. Imre, catching sight of them, waved and nudged his way through the crowd.

"You look so elegant!" Szerena gushed.

Imre grinned. Gisella could tell he was pleased. "Your lilac branch, Imre . . ." she said softly. "It was beautiful. It was so nice of you to make it for me — for us. . . ."

"A lilac branch? I don't know anything about a lilac branch."

"Oh, come on, Imre," Szerena cried, giggling. "You know very well it was you who put it on our gate."

Imre smiled down on them. "Maybe the good angel put it there."

The music started again. Imre's arm encircled the waist of a blond-haired, blue-eyed girl close by and swept her away with him. "A newfound cousin!" he called back over his shoulder, grinning.

On and on the music played. Dance followed dance till it was time for a rest. Now the musicians played a *hallgato*, a listening song. The young folks formed small circles as the melody of the song flowed through the room. Arms entwined, they swayed gently to and fro:

> *I shall be a tree, if you are its blossoms.*
> *I shall be a flower, if you are the dew.*
> *I shall be the dew, if you are the sunshine,*
> *so that our bodies and souls shall unite.*

When the song was ended, the dancing resumed with pauses in between for other *hallgatos* and drinks of cold beer.

All too soon, Mama appeared. "It's getting late, girls. Time to go home."

Reluctantly, with many a backward glance, Szerena and Gisella followed her out. Arm in arm, they walked through the twilight down the road toward home.

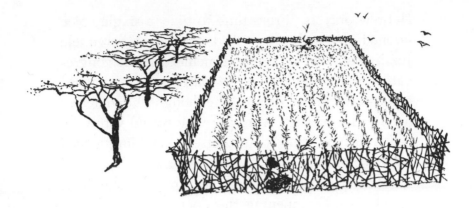

SEVEN

ORDINARILY, only men and boys attended Saturday morning services at the synagogue. Women and girls came at very special times, like the High Holy Days. This Saturday morning, however, the women's section was fully occupied.

Gisella felt uncomfortable on the hard synagogue bench. It was so high, her feet couldn't reach the floor. After a while, she could feel pins and needles pricking her soles. She slipped forward to the very edge and pressed her toes against the wooden floor.

Through the open transom of the door separating them from the men's section, came the male voices rising and falling as they chanted the solemn

75

Hebrew prayers. From time to time, a single voice intoned above the rest. It belonged to her uncle Jozsi. It was an honor for a member of the congregation to be called up to the platform to read aloud a portion from the Torah. The thought flitted across her mind — if Papa were here, he would surely be called up, too. She found herself imagining a serious-looking Papa with a prayer shawl.

Szerena was shaking her by the shoulder. "Look! They're opening the doors!"

There was a sudden stir among the children. Smiles replaced the grave expressions on the faces of the grown-ups. The door was now wide open, and Gisella spotted Cousin Kalman seated beside his two elder brothers, Jena and Sandor. Catching sight of her, Kalman stuck his tongue out at her. She paid him back by making a funny face.

From the platform, the rabbi announced, "Janos Weiss, stand up so everybody can see you!"

Friendly hands pulled the blushing young man from his seat and shoved him toward the front. He stood there, shy and abashed. The rabbi came down and put his arm around the young man's shoulder. "Think of it!" he said. "Our own little Janos all grown-up and going to be married to Erzsi. A prettier, more pious mistress of a house, nobody could ask for! Janos, may God grant you both much happiness and a good sweet life!"

The blessing was a signal, for instantly from all directions, candy, raisins, and nuts came flying at

Janos. With each throw, the men shouted, "May you have a good sweet life!" And the women echoed, "As sweet as these good things!"

Whooping with delight, the youngsters tore down on the groom-to-be, almost knocking him over. There was a mad scramble. In no time, there wasn't a sweet to be found.

"Look at all we got!" Gisella and Szerena cried jubilantly.

"My!" Mama exclaimed. "You've collected enough for a whole sweet year yourselves. Better not eat any of it now. You'll spoil your appetite for the good Sabbath meal."

Meanwhile, Janos was being thumped on the back and showered with good wishes. People laughed and made good-natured jokes. Then with many exchanges of "A good Sabbath!" the congregation dispersed.

"I didn't see Erzsi," Szerena remarked as they were walking home.

"It's the custom. She'll get her congratulations this evening," replied Mama. "The bride-to-be always invites the women to her house. And we'll have something sweet there, too, because Erzsi's mother will serve tea and cake."

Gisella looked at the goodies in her hand. "Szerena," she said, "don't you wish they'd announce a wedding every week?"

Gisella was in the attic, where it was always

cool and twilight-shadowy. By early fall, it would be crammed full with all the good things stored away for the long winter — dried beans, barley, rye, all kinds of dried fruits, each item neatly heaped in its own pile on the wooden floor. There would be corn, too, many bunches of yellow-brown cobs hanging on sticks. At this time, the end of May, the attic was nearly empty. But a sweet, slightly burned smell still lingered in the air.

She bent down to pick up a few prunes to nibble on. Something white behind the bushel baskets caught her eye. Pushing them aside, she found a long white cardboard box. What was it doing there? she wondered. She lifted the lid and peeked inside. Shoes! The loveliest pair of little girl's shoes. They were black, with a sheen so brilliant, she could almost see her face in them. Each had a narrow little strap which buttoned across the instep and was lined with cream-colored material. Whose shoes were they?

She stared down at her own brown sandals. They looked so heavy and clumsy by comparison. A dainty pair of shoes like these would be fun to dance in. And they would go perfectly with her Sabbath dress! It was bright red with splashes of big white roses. Mama had made it out of a piece of cloth left over from some curtains.

In a jiffy, the brown sandals were off. She slipped her right foot into the new shoe. Her toes squeezed in, but her heel wouldn't follow. It had to fit! She set her teeth obstinately. It just had to! She pushed and pushed, and finally the shoes were buttoned over her feet. She stood up in a sweat, her pinched toes protesting painfully. Moving about was sheer agony, but how slim and elegant her feet looked!

Gingerly she climbed down the ladder, holding tight to the rungs for the soles were very slippery. She hobbled across the front room and out the door.

Mama was on her knees inspecting the kitchen garden. Every step was torture, but Gisella was determined to have Mama see the shoes on her feet. She knew if she once took them off, she'd never be able to get them on again.

She went limping to Mama's side. "I found them in the attic," she said, pointing to the shoes. "Aren't they beautiful?"

Mama sat back on her heels. "They are. Papa sent them from America. It's a special kind of shiny leather they make there."

"Oh, Mama, I just adore them!" Gisella wailed. "Only they're too small!"

"I know."

"Then why didn't you let me wear them when my feet were littler," Gisella complained, "instead of hiding them away in the attic?"

"They came only about a month ago. It was in the morning when you were both in school. The minute I laid eyes on them, I could see they wouldn't fit. Your papa made a mistake." A sad smile wavered across her mouth. "I knew it would make you unhappy, so I thought it would be better if you never saw them. I meant to give them away to some neighbor's child, but there's always so much to do, I forgot." She looked up at Gisella, her eyes full of sympathy. "Better take them off, my child. I can see they're hurting your feet."

Gisella was both sorry and relieved to remove them. Her poor cramped toes were all red. Gratefully they spread themselves apart on the cool, spongy earth. "Maybe we should give them to Ilka Neni's daughter, Ibolja. She's only five. Her feet are little," she said glumly. She ran her fingers slowly over the shiny, smooth leather.

"Don't take it so to heart," Mama said. "When we get to America, I'm sure Papa will be glad to buy you a pair just like them. So put them away where you found them and go help Szerena in the flax field."

As she buckled on her sandals, Gisella could not help but think — if one can buy wonderful shoes like these in America, perhaps it wouldn't be too bad living there. Only — to go away — to leave this place . . . . No, she decided firmly, my sandals are good enough. They are very comfortable.

When Gisella came out again, Mama had left the garden and was sitting quietly in the lush green grass at the back of the house. Her hands were folded in her lap, and her face was as peaceful and calm as the Sabbath day itself. It's good to have a Sabbath, Gisella told herself. It gives Mama a chance to rest.

Nearby, their brown and white cow seemed to be celebrating the Sabbath, too. Weekday mornings, Andrus, the cowherd, drove the village cows to the pasture, returning them in the evening. But on Saturdays, their cow remained on their own ground. She ate leisurely of the grass, the bell around her neck responding with every slow swish of her tail.

"I just want to say hello to the cow, Mama," Gisella said. "Then I'll go sit with Szerena."

The cow lifted her head as Gisella approached. Her brown eyes fixed themselves on the little girl. Gisella stroked the sleek furred head. "You nice sweet cow!" she purred. "You good cow!"

The cow lowered her head and pulled away abruptly from Gisella's caressing hand.

"What's the matter . . . ?"

Gisella had no time to finish. The cow let out a loud, rumbling moo. Its head came up sharply, and the curved horns caught hold of Gisella's dress. The next thing Gisella knew, she was being pitched high in the air! The trees — the sky — the whole world was toppling! She was falling — falling! Kerplop! Amazingly, right smack into Mama's lap!

For a moment, Mama and Gisella sat dazed, unable to comprehend just what had occurred. Mama finally found her voice. "Are you all right?

81

Are you all right?"

Gisella stared up into Mama's astonished face. "I'm fine," she uttered a bit shakily.

"It's a miracle!" Mama cried, throwing her arms around Gisella. "You might have landed on a stone, or even the fence! What's come over that creature?" She jumped up and approached warily. But the cow was once again its docile self, munching away contentedly on a tender clump of grass.

Mama stood there nonplussed. "She's never done anything like that before."

"Maybe she doesn't like me to pet her anymore," Gisella said ruefully.

"Oh, I know what it is!" Mama exclaimed. "Your dress! It's such a bright red it startled her."

"But, Mama, I thought cows are supposed to be color-blind."

Mama laughed with relief. "I guess this one isn't. Anyway, so long as you weren't hurt, it doesn't matter. But, hereafter, better keep out of her way when you're wearing red."

The flax field lay just beyond the kitchen garden. It was bordered by a fence woven of cut branches to keep out the chickens and geese. Inside the fence, Szerena was sitting on the ground wielding a long switch to discourage any sparrow or starling from alighting.

Gisella clambered over the fence, picked up another switch, and seated herself at the opposite end of the field. As she whipped her switch back and forth, she shouted across to Szerena the tale of her unexpected tumble through the air. It sent them both into gales of laughter.

Next to the flax field was the plum orchard. Row upon row of umbrellalike trees were covered with delicate pink and white blossoms, their heavy sweetness perfuming the air. If I have to sit in one place, Gisella thought, how much nicer to be under one of those plum trees looking up at a lovely roof of flowers overhead. She heaved a bored sigh. In just a couple more days, the flax seeds would start sprouting. Then the thieving birds would give up. But now the field must be watched every minute until sundown. Back and forth, back and forth sailed the switch. No bird was going to get away with a single seed. Not while she was there!

Swish, swish! To and fro, to and fro. Change from right hand to left. Swish, swish. Left hand to right. Minutes turned into hours. The afternoon dragged on endlessly. Weary of talk, the girls fell silent.

Gisella's head swung back in a wide yawn. Would the sun never set? Would the birds never go back to their nests to sleep? How lucky we had Imre chasing the birds while we were in the synagogue. I couldn't have put up with this for the whole day, she thought.

EIGHT

June days were hot and sunny, and there
was no need for shoes. Gisella and her friends Ilona
and Juli sat on the porch wriggling their bare toes
in the moist brown earth. "I know what we can
do," suggested Gisella. "Let's go dangle our feet in
the ditch."

All along the streets of Helmecz there were
ditches for drawing off the rain to keep the roads
dry. In front of each house, a small footbridge
spanned the ditch, for they were seldom without
water.

The girls plopped themselves down on the little
bridge and started splashing about. Juli reached
down into the water and scooped up a handful

84

of mud. "See!" she said. "There are snails in this ditch. Let's sing the snail song."

When each girl had a snail in her hand, they began singing:

> *Snail, Uncle Snail,*
> *Put out your little head,*
> *And I will give you*
> *A big piece of bread.*
>
> *Here come the Tartars!*
> *They'll chop off your head,*
> *Toss you in a salty well*
> *And throw thorns upon your head.*

The snail in Gisella's hand timidly poked its pale gray head out of the shell. Gisella was certain her singing had coaxed it out.

The snail felt cool and soft on her skin, but a moment later, it retreated into its home. She held it up to her eye and peered into the narrow opening trying to discover what went on inside. She sang to it again, but the snail remained inside. After a while, she gave up and tossed it back into the ditch.

Whistling cheerily, a young boy came sauntering up the street. "Hello, Cousin Kalman," Gisella called out.

"Hello," he returned, grinning down at them. "What are you girls doing?"

Gisella shrugged. "Oh, just splashing."

"Say, you ought to see our mulberry trees!" Kalman said. "They're getting so full of leaves!"

"You'll have lots of delicious mulberries," Ilona told him.

"I wasn't thinking about them. I was thinking about the silkworms. They'll have plenty of juicy leaves to feed on."

"The man from the silk factory in Ungwar is bringing the worms tomorrow," Juli said.

"I know," Ilona chimed in. "They're opening the schoolhouse especially so they can give them out."

"You going to take any?" asked Gisella.

Ilona's nose crinkled up snootily. "Not me!"

"I am!" Kalman declared. "I'm going to take a whole bunch of them. They will pay good money for the cocoons."

"I wonder why they're doing this?" Gisella said. "They never asked us before."

Kalman tried to lift a pebble with his bare toes. "Some kind of experiment, I guess. They don't ask the grown-ups because they're too busy. But it's easy to take care of the worms, so they figure maybe the children can do it."

"Szerena wants me to help her raise them," Gisella said. "But we have just one mulberry tree. Its trunk is long and skinny, and the leaves are way up high. It would be hard for us to reach them."

"You can always come and get some branches from our trees," offered Kalman. "Or, if you like, I'll climb up that old tree of yours and cut off some branches whenever you need them."

"Oh, would you, Kalman?"

"Anytime. I can climb a tree like a squirrel," he boasted. "Well, I have to go. I have to fill up the wood pails for my mother."

"It's getting pretty late," Ilona decided. "I'd better get on home, too."

Juli scrambled to her feet. "I'll go with you."

Her friends went away, but Gisella still idled on the little footbridge. From a distance, she could hear a fluttering chorus of cowbells approaching. Was it that late?

Szerena came out of the house. Gisella went to meet her, and together they waited at the front gate for their cow.

Gisella's upturned face looked toward the horizon. Already the setting sun was sweeping a feathery scarf of rose and violet across the sky. "It could never be as lovely as this in America, could it?" she murmured.

"The sky is beautiful everywhere," Szerena replied. "But Papa lives in New York City. Think of that! The largest city in the whole world! That's what I would like!"

Gisella glanced at her sister. She sounded so eager. "Szerena," she asked, "doesn't it bother you at all about leaving here?"

Szerena smiled. "A big change is always a bit scary. Especially when you're not sure what things are really like in the new place. Still, I wouldn't want to give up the chance for anything! I don't want to be stuck on a poor farm all of my life!"

The cows came in sight, led by Andrus and his big staff, a large cloud of dust trailing behind them. Slowly they trudged past, each animal finding its own way home. Now their cow was nudging the gate with her forehead. Szerena lifted the latch and let her in.

The following day Gisella and Szerena brought home a bowlful of silkworms. "We can keep them in here," Szerena said, leading the way into the storage room, which at this season of the year was the summer kitchen. "Bring the long tray," she added. "The one with the little legs."

True to his promise, Kalman had supplied them with enough leaves and twigs to completely cover the tray. They carefully sprinkled the worms over this greenery.

"You'd never think they were worms!" Gisella exclaimed. "They look more like poppy seeds."

"Wait till they start growing. They'll look like worms then all right," replied Szerena.

"Won't they climb off the tray and fall on the floor? There's nothing to hold them."

"No. The man said they would cling to the twigs and just eat and eat."

Thereafter, first thing every morning the girls

ran to examine the tray. It was amazing how quickly the teeny specks were turning into wriggly threadlike worms. The leaves were eaten full of holes. Again and again they had to be replenished with fresh ones. By the end of the month, the worms had thickened and grown tremendously.

Kalman came around one afternoon to inspect their batch. "Hmm! They're way bigger than mine." He scratched his head. "Why is that?"

On hearing this, the sisters paid a visit to his house to see for themselves. Indeed it was true. Kalman's worms just couldn't compare in length and fatness to theirs.

Kalman scowled down on his trays. "Here I've been giving you the best of care, the finest mulberry leaves in the whole village, and just look at you!"

"It is odd," Szerena made her voice sound sympathetic, but over Kalman's head, she shot a triumphant glance at Gisella.

Kalman frowned down on the worms. "Maybe I could stretch them a little."

"Oh, no!" protested Gisella. "You'll hurt them!"

"I'll be careful." Gently Kalman tried pulling on a worm. It was no use. It stretched just so far, and when he let go, it immediately settled back to its original shape. Kalman appeared baffled. "You girls were just lucky, I guess. Your batch of worms was probably healthier to begin with."

The sisters did not bother to contradict him.

They just smiled. They were convinced that they could raise silkworms better than any boy.

By about the end of the fifth week, the girls hung the branches from a shelf. The worms, transformed into nice fat caterpillars, had stopped eating. As they hung from the branches, each wiggled around and around. With silken threads which exuded from their mouths, they were spinning cocoons about themselves. Shaped somewhat like peanut shells, they were mostly white, but a few were a delicate pink-orange or egg-shell blue.

On an appointed day, the man from the silk factory came trundling a large barrel and scale. Szerena and Gisella held their breaths as he weighed their pile of cocoons.

"Well," the man smiled at Mama, "your daughters have done a fine job!" Into Szerena's palm, he laid a koruna.

"Oh, thank you!" the girls gasped. They could hardly believe their eyes.

Szerena proudly gave Mama the money.

Gisella laughed happily. "Next year, Szerena, we ought to raise two trays instead of one!"

"Next year?" For an instant, Szerena had a faraway look in her eyes. "Next year at this time, we will be in America."

Gisella didn't say anything. She didn't even want to think about it.

Another letter from Papa said things were going

well. Soon they would all be together again. . . .

Gisella gazed up into Mama's careworn face, now transformed with the brightness of hope. Papa was forever holding out the dazzling promise of their going to America. Would they? Somehow Gisella could not quite believe it.

There were times when she even doubted that there was a Papa. She wondered about that. Was it because she had been too young to remember him? Or was it that through all the troubled years, they talked so little about him? Always he seemed unreal to her.

But America seemed real enough. The way people were always talking about America, it must be a wonderland! The marvelous things that Papa sent them from there!

Gisella stretched out on the wooden settee. Head hanging back over the edge, she lay with half-closed eyes, dreaming about America.

NINE

IN THE BROAD FIELDS to the east of town, each villager had his own small plot where he grew wheat, rye, barley, corn, and potatoes. Mama would trek to her field regularly throughout the hot summer days. Often Szerena and Gisella went along to help with the weeding. But mostly, the girls busied themselves around the house and barn and tended the kitchen garden at the back of the house. As the weeks rolled on, the blazing sun gradually burned their skin and bleached Gisella's hair to an even lighter gold.

Early in the summer wild strawberries grew in abundance on the slope near the schoolhouse. There the girls would scramble about of an afternoon with the other village children, filling pails with the tiny fruit to bring home.

Summertime — it was wonderful to sink one's teeth into the delicious yellow-pink fruit from their lone peach tree, or munch on juicy purple plums from the orchard. There were small red currants and furry soft raspberries ready to be picked. These they ate to bursting, then helped Mama turn the rest into mouth-watering conserves and jellies.

Sometimes, when chores were done, Gisella would slip off by herself to the back pasture. She would stretch out on the tall, velvety grass, dotted with golden buttercups. Enveloped in drowsy peacefulness, she would gaze up steadily at the clear blue sky. The only sound invading the stillness might be the occasional buzz of an insect flitting by. Or she and Szerena would climb up to the low flat branch of the quince tree. It was pleasant sitting there in the shade, looking out over the garden now ablaze with color. There were asters in all shades — white, blue, purple, and fuchsia — and bright red bleeding hearts. In one corner was a little bush which people called *Isten Faja* (God's Tree). When its evergreenlike leaves were pressed between the fingers, they gave forth a heavenly scent.

When the day was especially torrid, Mama allowed them to go swimming with their friends in the river which meandered along the edge of the village. They would splash and tumble about in

their pinafores, whooping with delight. At the
shallow end, a crude bridge of wooden planks
spanned the river. It shook and bounced perilously
with each step. Though she tried not to show it,
Gisella was frightened every time she had to cross
it. She envied Szerena, who could skip back and
forth with unconcern.

On the opposite side, the river was banked
by some high mounds of yellow clay. Someone
would shout, "Come on! Let's go sliding!" Immediately the youngsters would wet down a clay hill
until its smooth surface made a perfect slide. As
they coasted down, pinafores and bottoms would
turn a bright yellow. "It doesn't matter," Gisella
would cry. "Slide, slide! It washes off!"

Late in July a dealer drove up from the city
with his wagon and helpers to pick the plums in
the orchard.

"Oh, Mama, did you sell him the whole crop?"
Gisella asked anxiously.

"Of course not," Mama assured her, laughing.
"I left two laden trees for us. That should be plenty
for you. We'll start drying the plums and making
lechwar tomorrow. Imre will bring us some heavy
roots and tree stumps for the fires."

"Is anyone coming to help?" inquired Szerena.

"Zali Neni, of course. And Muncie Neni, too."

Gisella gave a joyous little skip. It was always
great fun when Zali Neni and Muncie Neni came
to help.

The following day, right after lunch, the girls trudged to the well at the foot of their street with their water buckets. The round, moss-covered wall of the well barely reached to Gisella's waist. Fearfully she peered down. A person could easily topple in. She made sure to back away as Szerena lowered the bucket.

The constant drawing of water always kept the earth around the well soggy. It was a sunny day, and clouds of little butterflies of an exquisite blue hovered above the wetness. Gisella watched them, fascinated. They made the ground look like a piece of sky, she thought.

When they got back, Imre was already digging out the drying pits. Along came Zali Neni and Muncie Neni hauling a huge cauldron between them.

"I appreciate your bringing the big kettle," Mama said.

Zali Neni waved her hand. Her round face dimpled. "Of course, Muncie Neni and I are expecting a tiny bit of *lechwar* from you in return."

"Me, too," added Imre.

"Naturally," Mama replied. "It should only turn out good."

"You know your plum preserve is always delicious," Muncie Neni said.

Zali Neni rolled up her sleeves. "Enough of talk. Let's get to work."

Mama brought out a nest of baskets. Then all proceeded to the orchard to pluck the plums from the trees she had reserved. Next they carried the filled baskets to the drying pits. At the bottom of the first pit, Imre had set a stump to burning, banking the fire with heavy roots to keep it smouldering. Across the top, flush with the ground, Mama set a bed of tightly woven branches, and on this, the women piled high a heap of plums.

The girls meanwhile were washing the plums set aside for the *lechwar*. Zali Neni came over. "Here, let me at them," she said, plunging her chubby arms into the pails of water and scooping up armfuls of the purple fruit. Plop! Plop! She tossed them into a clean basket, and immediately all fell to pitting them. The pitted plums were then dumped into the cauldron.

At the second pit, Imre fanned the burning pile of logs into flame. Carefully, he lowered the loaded cauldron onto the logs.

"Stand back!" he warned as Gisella and Szerena approached. "If you girls fall into the pot, the *lechwar* will be too sweet." With a grin and a wave, he departed.

"We have to go home, too, and get supper for our families," Muncie Neni said.

"Yes," added Zali Neni. "We'll be back later to spell you off with the stirring through the night."

But Mama and the girls continued to stay with the fires. Already a pleasant smoky sweetness was being wafted on the air. From time to time, Mama stirred the plums stewing in the cauldron with a large wooden paddle, while the girls raked the plums drying at the other hole.

"Want supper?" Mama called out.

"Oh, yes! I'm starving!" Gisella cried.

"So am I!" echoed Szerena. "We've been so busy I almost forgot about eating."

"All right, then, I'll get it ready. Gisella, you go and pull up some lettuce, and, Szerena, you stay here. Make sure you stir the mixture regularly. We don't want the plums to stick to the bottom of the pot and burn. And also keep an eye on the drying plums."

Soon Mama was back with a bowl of cut up lettuce, scallions, and thin slices of white radish, topped with thick sour cream. They sat down close by the fires and helped themselves from the bowl in between bites of thick slices of black bread. A large cup of cool milk completed their meal.

The lingering summer sun had begun to set by the time the aunts returned. Together they watched and stirred and shifted the drying plums about, laughing and talking all the while.

"You're all going to stay up the whole night. Can we do it too?" Gisella begged.

Mama nodded. "If you think you can."

On hearing this, the girls rushed off to the house and dragged out their bedding. The night air was turning chilly. It felt cozy sitting in the firelight with the warm coverlet tucked around them.

"How about some tea and cake?" suggested Mama.

"Tea is fine," Muncie Neni replied. "But instead of cake, if I could just have a small piece of that nice white bread you Jewish women bake for your Sabbath?"

"You mean hallah," Mama said, pleased. "Luckily I still have some left over from Saturday. You're more than welcome."

The hot tea was especially good with the big slices of hallah spread with raspberry jelly.

"How about one of your stories, Muncie Neni?" Mama said. "You tell such good ones."

"A story! A story!" the others chimed in.

Muncie Neni shuffled the drying plums. For a moment her gaze followed a thin trail of smoke curling upward.

Once there was somewhere in this world a peasant who had three daughters. One fine day, he got ready to go to the town fair. I will bring back a present for each of my daughters, he said to himself. But first I must find out how much they love me.

So he asked the eldest, and she said, "I love you, Father, as much as I love the most beautiful dress that one can buy in town."

And the second daughter said, "I love you, Father, as much as I love a dress all covered with diamonds."

"And you, Marya, my youngest, how much do you love me?" the father asked.

And Marya replied, "Dearest Father, I love you as much as I love salt in my soup."

The father grew very angry. "Salt in your soup!" he

cried. "You ungrateful girl! Is that all I mean to you? Get out of my house. I don't want any daughter who cares so little for me!"

Poor Marya was very sad. Where could she go? To whom could she turn? She packed her things in a little bundle and went out into the wide, wide world.

For days she wandered about, till at last she came to the palace of a very rich king. The king's minister felt sorry for her. "We would like to give you some work," he said. "But the only work we can give you is that of goose girl."

"I will be glad to be the goose girl," she said, "if only you let me stay here."

So she became the goose girl and lived in the kingdom in wretched misery.

Every night Marya had to go to the palace kitchen for her food. One day as she waited for her portion, the cook grew very cross. "Get out of my way, you dirty ragamuffin!" he shouted. "I don't want any of your dirt getting into my dishes. Be off with you!"

Quickly Marya grabbed up her portion and ran out of the kitchen. As she passed by a window of the palace, she looked in and saw the king's son washing his face. "Where is my prince going?" she asked.

The prince replied. "I go where I please, ragged goose girl. And tonight I choose to go to the Silver Ball. Be gone from my window!"

Marya went back to the goosehouse and opened the parcel of food the cook had given her. As she ate, big tears rolled down her cheeks. All at once she heard a tiny squeak. Looking around, she saw that a little mouse had popped out of a hole. She was sorry for the poor little thing, so she fed him a morsel of her bread.

The mouse was very grateful. He darted back into his hole and brought out a walnut which he dropped at Marya's feet. Then he disappeared into his hole again.

Marya picked up the nut and looked into an opening at one end. There she saw something shiny. She reached in and pulled, and out of the shell came the most beautiful silver gown that ever was!

How happy the goose girl was! Now I can go to the ball, too, she decided. Quickly she washed herself, combed her hair, and put on the wonderful silver gown. Then she began to sing:

> *Mist before me!*
> *Mist behind me!*
> *No one see me.*
> *No one find me!*

And she hurried off to the ball.

You can imagine the excitement that the magnificently dressed stranger caused at the ball! She was so beautiful, everyone wanted to dance with her. But the prince wouldn't let them. He wanted to keep her all to himself. "Who are you?" he kept on asking. "Where do you come from?"

But the girl only answered, "I come from No-Towel Castle."

So they danced together all through the night. The prince said he would see her home, but when he turned away for a moment, she slipped out and ran all the way back to the goosehouse.

She put the gown back into the nutshell, and the next day she was back tending the geese clad in her dirty rags.

That evening she went to the kitchen as usual for her supper. "You here again, you filthy creature!" the cook screamed. He threw some scraps at her. "Take your portion and get out!"

Poor Marya crept away. But when she was outside, she passed the prince's window again. This time the prince was combing his hair.

"Where is my prince going tonight?" she asked.

"Where I go is no business of yours, ragged goose girl," the prince replied. "But if you must know, I am going to the Gold Ball. Now get away from my window!"

The girl ran back to the goosehouse. Quickly she

pulled out the dress from the nutshell, and lo and behold, instead of silver, it was now pure gold!

At once Marya washed, combed her hair, and put on the gold dress. Then she began to sing:

Mist before me!
Mist behind me!
No one see me.
No one find me!

And she hurried off to the ball.

The prince was sitting sadly all by himself. But the minute he caught sight of the girl in the golden gown, a happy smile spread across his face. He rushed over to her and asked her to dance with him. They danced and danced, and all the while he kept begging her to tell him where she came from. But all the girl would say was, "I'm from No-Comb Castle."

"Tonight you must let me see you home!" the prince cried, but the minute his back was turned, the goose girl slipped away.

Back in the goosehouse, she carefully folded up the gold gown and put it into the nutshell. In the morning, looking her ragged self again, Marya drove the geese out to pasture.

That night, when she went to the kitchen for her food, the cross cook threw her supper at her. "Out! Out you filthy thing!" he yelled.

Again she stopped at the prince's window. The prince was all dressed up. "I see my prince is getting ready for the Diamond Ball," she said.

"What if I am, you insolent goose girl. Stop poking your nose into my affairs!" he shouted angrily. He picked up his hand mirror and threw it at her.

Ah, Marya said to herself, this time I'll make sure to get to the ball before he does. Back to the goosehouse she went. This time the dress inside the nutshell was made of shiny white satin covered with diamonds! How it sparkled!

In no time at all, Marya had washed, combed her hair, and put on the dress. Then once again she sang:

Mist before me!
Mist behind me!
No one see me.
No one find me!

And she hurried off to the ball.

When the prince arrived, the goose girl was already dancing with someone else. But the prince snatched her away. All evening he kept her to himself, for by now he was madly in love with her. Over and over he begged, "Tell me truthfully, where do you come from? I have asked everyone in the palace, but no one has ever heard of the places you mentioned."

The goose girl only laughed and said, "I come from No-Mirror Castle."

The prince took off his ring and put it on her finger. "Promise me you will wear this ring forever and ever," he said.

She only smiled, and before the night was over, the beautiful girl had slipped away.

The unhappy prince searched for her everywhere, but alas, he could not find her. All through the next day, he moped around in the palace speaking to no one. The king and queen tried to cheer him up, but it was no use.

The next night the goose girl tarried near the kitchen until the cook's back was turned. Quick as a flash, she sneaked into the kitchen, took off the ring, and dropped it into the soup being prepared for the royal supper.

When the soup was being served, the ladle clinked against something hard. The servant lifted the ladle, and there was the ring! The prince cried out in astonishment, "That's my ring! The one I gave to the most beautiful girl at the ball! Summon the cook!"

When the cook appeared, the prince shouted, "Who was in your kitchen when you prepared this soup?"

The cook was frightened. He thought that the ragged goose girl must have gotten some dirt in the pot. "Er — why — nobody, your Majesty," he stammered.

"If you don't tell me who was in your kitchen, you will

be hung!" the prince shouted. "But if you tell the **truth**, then I promise no harm will come to you."

The cook dropped to his knees. "It was only the goose girl, sire," he confessed, trembling.

"The goose girl!" cried the prince. "Go and fetch her here at once!"

But the goose girl was ready for him. She had washed herself, combed her hair, and put on the diamond dress. When she came into the palace, the prince was overjoyed. He threw his arms around her. "This maiden will be my wife!" he said to the king and queen.

They began preparing for the wedding immediately. Naturally Marya asked the prince to invite her father and her two sisters. Then she went to the kitchen and told the cook to prepare a special dish just for her father but to leave out all the salt.

At last it was the night of the wedding. The bride's father, even though he still felt hurt, was glad to see his daughter again.

Then they served the wedding supper, but the poor father hardly ate a thing.

"What's the matter, Father?" asked Marya. "Is there something wrong with the food?"

"No, my daughter. The food is very well prepared," the father answered. "But I can't eat it because there's not a drop of salt in it."

Marya looked at her father, and she said, "Father, do you remember when you asked me how much I loved you? when I replied, 'as much as I love the salt in my soup,' you thought I did not love you at all. Now you see that food without salt isn't worth anything."

"Yes, my daughter," the father said, with tears running down his cheeks. "Can you forgive me?"

"Of course, Father," said Marya. "Anyway, it has all turned out for the best. If you had not driven me away, I might never have found my prince."

So that's how the goose girl became a princess. And Marya and the prince lived happily for a long, long time.

And if they haven't died, they are still living happily to this very day.

Szerena sighed drowsily. "If only such things could really happen."

Wagging a finger at her, Muncie Neni chanted:

My tale is done.
You've had your fun.
If you doubt it's true,
Go eat your shoe.

Gisella stretched under the warm cover. The night sky was sprinkled with countless twinkling lights. In one corner, just above a tall tree, hung the moon, an orange-yellow ball. Gisella gazed through drooping lids at the women huddled by the fire, their shawls drawn over their shoulders. Their voices were soft and murmuring. Was another tale being told?

Zali Neni's voice seemed to come from far away. "So it looks as if you're really going."

"Yes," was Mama's reply. "In the letter — it just arrived this week — Herschel says we should figure on next year."

"But when exactly?"

"Well, there are still things to settle —much to arrange. But by early spring, I imagine. . . ." Mama's voice drifted away.

In the morning, Gisella awoke to find herself lying in her own bed. She realized the women must have carried her into the house. Quickly she dressed and rushed out of doors. "Good morning," she called out.

"Good morning, sleepyhead!" everyone responded.

"See, Gisella, we're all finished," Szerena said, motioning to the big heap of wrinkled black prunes.

"And the *lechwar* came out just perfect," added Zali Neni.

Mama pointed proudly to the row of white earthenware *lechwar* pots filled to the brim with the dark jellied mixture. "Thanks to your help, Zali and Muncie Neni. You mustn't forget to call on me when you're ready to make your own."

"Don't worry, we will," they told her, smiling.

"Umm!" Szerena smacked her lips. "When I think of all the yummy things Mama can make now! Cake and filled kreplach (triangular shaped envelopes of dough), and especially *lechwar* with noodles!"

Gisella suddenly felt very hungry. "I could eat some right this minute!"

"Let's get the prunes and the *lechwar* up into the attic," Mama said. "Then I'll fix breakfast for all of us."

TEN

As August days gave way to each other, the ripened grain turned to gold in the fields. There was but one threshing machine in all of Helmecz. In return for a portion of the yield, its owner drove it from one plot to another helping the families harvest their crops.

In their own field, Mama and Szerena followed after the thresher making sure to gather up every scrap of the gleanings. The harvested grain was brought to the miller for grinding. His payment was a share of the flour. At the start of each day, Szerena drove the geese into the reaped fields to graze on whatever was left.

In the flax field, the plants were already more

106

than three feet high. "See how many have the little white flowers," Mama rejoiced. "That means the finest linen."

On the first windy morning, Mama said, "It looks like a good day for flailing the flax. Gisella, today you take the geese so that Szerena can work with me."

Gisella's little body stiffened. Oh, Mama, do I have to? The question almost sprang from her lips.

Mama and Szerena set off for the flax field carrying a long-handled scythe and flailing sticks, while a worried Gisella began rounding up the flock. With the aid of a long switch, she urged the geese down the garden path and out into the street. They waddled along, honking and hissing and stretching their long necks.

Slowly they marched past the small houses, all alike with their thatched roofs and walls of part whitewash and part blue. The road ahead was splashed with sunshine. Birds were singing, and the air was filled with many scents. But Gisella scarcely noticed. She could think only of the fear that simmered inside her.

It was safe enough here in the village. But already she was approaching its end. Just ahead was the last house. Would the strange old man be on the porch again?

She tried not to think of the fearsome tale Kalman had related about that old man. "You know what he did once?" Kalman had whispered in great excitement. "He tried to kill himself!"

"Oh, Kalman!"

"Yes, he did!" Kalman was emphatic. "He hung himself from a beam in the ceiling of that very house!"

"But, Kalman, that's silly. He's alive!"

"I know. But he would have died if it hadn't been for his daughter. She found him just in time. She started screaming, and the neighbors came running and cut him down."

"But why, Kalman? Why did he do it?"

"I don't know. They say he's a little crazy. Ever since that time he sits in his rocking chair and just stares."

"I don't believe it. You're just making the whole thing up to frighten me."

"It's all true! Every word of it! I heard the women talking."

Gisella had never been sure whether Kalman had told her the truth. As she passed by the house, she averted her face, but her eyes could not help taking a quick glance.

He was there — the strange old man with the long, straggly white hair falling over his shoulders. He kept rocking, rocking endlessly, and his vacant eyes seemed to be staring straight through her. Gisella's shoulders hunched. Her breath quickened. She squeezed her eyes tight to shut out the image. She had to get away from here! Terrified, she rushed the geese forward.

The road narrowed. To the left stretched a dense forest. The trees were so crowded that only pale slivers of sunlight filtered down, shrouding the road in perpetual gloom. The wind moaned and fluttered eerily through the topmost leaves.

Something equally scary lay in the hillside to the right, for here were the mysterious caves in which the villagers aged their wine. It did no good for Gisella to tell herself that she knew there were just barrels of wine in there. She could not quiet her fear. How do I know? I can't be absolutely sure. Horrible creatures like witches and hobgoblins always live in hidden places like these dark caves. Any minute now she expected to hear the squeak of hinges and the stealthy opening of a little cave door. The frightful things would spew forth, screeching and laughing with glee!

Gisella could almost feel their hot breath upon her; the grasp of their clammy claws on her quivering body. They were dragging her up there, pushing her through one of the doors and hurling her down, down, deep into the dark bowels of the earth! Once she was in their power, they would not let her go. Never again to see the light of day! Never again to see Mama or Szerena!

Panic possessed her! She found herself panting and yet not able to take in enough breath. She began to run, driving the geese before her. This set loose loud squawkings of protest from the flock. She was somewhat comforted by the familiar sound, but she kept on running, her bare feet heedless of the sharp rubble along the path.

She was past the forest — past the forbidding caves. She tried to calm herself. Nothing had happened. She was safe. But now a new terror loomed ahead — the cemetery!

If she could just get by that, everything would be all right. She shuddered. All the dead were in there. A brother and a sister were buried there since before Szerena was born, but every time she came by, she imagined she could hear them calling to her. Against her will, she found herself listening. She seemed to be all ears. Something sounded sort of whispery. What was it? Clapping her hands tightly over her ears, she went stumbling on.

At long last, the path opened wide. Before her, spread out like a huge checkerboard in the broad sunlight, were the squares of land belonging to the villagers. Gisella threw herself on the warm earth, trembling with relief. The geese were glad to stop their mad rushing and soon settled down to eating.

Gisella lay absolutely still as the bright sunshine seemed to penetrate into her very being, melting away all trace of her fright. You ought to be ashamed, she scolded herself. Acting like a baby scared to death of everything. Look at Szerena. She's been bringing the geese here every day since the reaping. She's not afraid. Well, maybe when I'm as old as Szerena, I'll be brave too.

Suddenly she recalled Mama saying that every

child has a guardian angel who watches over her all through the day and night. The thought heartened her. She sought out a shady spot at the field's edge, near a little stream, and sat watching the geese happily searching for leftover morsels.

Time passed peacefully. Gisella drowsed in the golden sunlight, while the geese ate their fill.

After a while, she looked up at the sky. It was getting late. Time to go home. Mama would be expecting her. Still she loitered. Guardian angel or no, she had to retrace her steps through the dreaded places.

She could put it off no longer. Clucking and calling, she rounded up the geese and once again pressed them forward with her stick. Finally she had them all on the road. She took a deep breath, stiffened her body resolutely, and plunged ahead.

The open fields were soon behind her. They were approaching the cemetery again. Suddenly the geese stretched their wings wide and started running furiously ahead! "No, geese! No!" Gisella screamed after them. "Don't you go off and leave me here alone!"

But even as she shouted, they disappeared in a cloud of brown dust. "What shall I do? I've lost the geese! What will Mama say?"

She ran and ran till her heart inside her ribs was beating like some wild thing. Past the caves, past the forest of trees she sped, her anxiety over the geese erasing all remembrance of the unknown terrors lurking along the way. She was past the old man's house, but there was still no sign of the geese! How was she ever going to face Mama?

Finally, she raced up the path to her house. "Mama!" she gasped. "The geese! They're gone! I tried — but — they — flew away!"

Mama's arms were around her. "It's all right, silly," she soothed. "They're here. The geese are all here. They're resting very nicely by the barn." Her dark eyes smiled down on the sobbing Gisella. "Don't you know you never have to worry about geese? They know their way home better than we do."

Gisella's small body gradually ceased trembling. Her tears ceased to flow. Everything that had happened seemed to melt away. Instead she found herself wondering — how did the geese know exactly which house was theirs?

"I worked pretty hard today," Szerena interrupted her thinking. "After helping Mama cut the flax, I beat and beat the stalks. My arms feel like they're dropping off. It was lucky there was a strong wind. It carried off the chaff straightaway. Well, there will be plenty of seeds for next year's planting. Only next year we won't have to bother because we won't be here. Mama will have to sell the seeds. After we eat," Szerena chattered on, "you can help us tie the stalks into bundles. After all, you had it easy all day just sitting around with the geese."

Easy! It was horrible! Gisella longed to scream out. But she held herself in check. She wasn't going to complain. She had fought off her fears. Wasn't that really being brave? She took a deep breath. Next time — maybe — she wouldn't be quite so scared.

Next morning Imre came with his wagon and carted the sheaths of flax to a marshy pool not far away. For ten days the bundles were left to soak in the stagnant water until the tough stalks grew soft and pliable. Then they were ready to be brought back home.

With skirts tied high above their knees, Mama and the girls waded barefoot into the water. Tiny water snakes slithered in every direction as they lifted the bundles. "Watch out for leeches!" Mama warned. "Don't let them stay on you too long!"

It was almost impossible to prevent the thick shiny worms from attaching themselves to one's legs. "A leech!" the girls would yell, and Mama would come instantly and carefully tear the leech off. The spot where it had clung itched. Sometimes it left a red mark or even a drop of blood.

When Imre finished piling up the dripping stalks onto his wagon, Mama joined him up front. The girls climbed onto the rear, feet dangling over the edge. As the horse clippety-clopped along the dirt road, the water dribbled through the floorboards and wove a thin wavy trail all the way home.

The following day Mama borrowed a flax chopper from a neighbor. This consisted of a narrow table at one end to which a long wooden knife or chopper was attached. While Gisella fed the chopper a few stalks at a time, Szerena worked the handle of the blade up and down, breaking apart the woody outside and releasing masses of grayish green and white threads. These were tied into bundles and piled on the ground like a heap of pony tails.

Next, with a comb made of long nails hammered through a piece of wood, they combed the pony tails till the threads lay straight and smooth. Finally, the threads were wound into skeins which Mama stored away in the attic.

On long winter evenings, when the women of the village were not busy with the canning, preserving, and drying of food, they would gather in one another's houses. Bringing their spindles, they would sit and gossip and spin the fibers to make them ready for weaving.

ELEVEN

A WHITE SILENCE had covered the landscape. Everything looked dazzlingly clean and un-
touched. Gisella and Szerena trudged through the
snow to the schoolhouse, each carrying schoolbooks
and a large piece of wood. The frosty air nipped at
their cheeks making them shine like rosy apples.

Zsiga was the monitor for the day. Stationed
at the door, he would not let them pass until he
brushed their high boots free of snow with a twig
broom. He seemed to be enjoying his task so much,
Gisella was envious. "I wish I could get to be monitor someday," she whispered to Szerena.

The fire in the potbellied stove was already
blazing. Throughout the school day, it would de-

115

vour chunk after chunk of wood. It was the children who kept the wood pails filled, for in order to gain admittance, each child had to bring a piece of firewood daily.

Usually the youngest pupils seated up front grew drowsy from the intense heat, while the oldest, like Szerena, in the back row, shivered from the cold drafts. Gisella was luckily in the middle and found it fairly comfortable.

Lessons commenced. The children of various ages bent over their work, each group waiting patiently for its turn to be heard. Clutching her pen, a frowning Gisella tried valiantly to form beautiful letters in her copybook. The teacher was very strict about penmanship.

Suddenly she heard the name "Kalman!" rip out. Up bobbed her head. Oh, dear, not again! Kalman was always getting into trouble. There he was, standing sullenly at the teacher's desk.

"Of course, you don't know," the teacher was saying sternly. "You haven't studied. By now, you should know your multiplication tables backwards and forwards."

She was a new teacher. She had been with them for only a few months. Gisella thought she was very pretty, with her round face and curly brown hair. But she didn't look a bit pretty now. She looked positively horrifying, her body drawn up so straight and tall, and her face set tight. She pointed toward the door. "Go and get a switch."

116

Kalman bundled himself up and shuffled out the door. A hush fell over the room as everyone waited.

In a few moments, he was back with a long branch. Without a word, he handed it to the teacher and bent over.

Chalks halted on slates. Pens and pencils remained poised as the children watched fearfully over the tops of their copybooks. The switch lashed across Kalman's backside. Swoosh! Swoosh! Swoosh! Each time Kalman hopped forward like a rabbit, but he didn't utter a sound.

Gisella winced with each blow. She could almost feel the pain whipping across her own back. Sobs began bubbling up out of her. Everyone turned to stare.

"Why are you crying?" The teacher demanded. "A boy who doesn't do his work deserves punishment. Get on with your work, or I shall have to punish you, too!"

Gisella dug her fists in her eyes, choked back the tears, and returned to her penmanship. Behind the teacher's back, Kalman flashed her a glance of gratitude.

Later, homeward bound, as the line of children walked two by two, Szerena whispered to Gisella, "That teacher! She gets you so scared, if she asked you how much is one and one, you wouldn't be able to answer! Am I glad I won't be back in this school next year! No matter what teachers are like in America, I'm sure they're not nearly so mean!"

All through the winter, the long evenings were enlivened by neighbors gathering at one another's homes to help with special chores. One night the women came to Mama's house to spin the flax. Hour after hour they sat, pulling on the threads with one hand and twisting them together with the other. The continuous threads were then wound on a spindle. Fingers had to be kept constantly moistened with the tongue. This interfered with talking, so Szerena read aloud favorite scary folktales from a storybook.

The little house was snug and warm. The heat from the stove lingered on in the thick walls, and the double sets of windows helped to shut out the cold. Lying in bed, Gisella listened raptly while her eyes dwelled on the shadows which, in the flickering light of the lamps, bobbed weirdly along the walls. They seemed frightening, even witchlike. Gisella was both sorry and relieved when the evening task came to an end.

Next day Mama took the spun yarn to the woman whose loom did all the weaving for the village. It took weeks, but finally Mama got back a tablecloth, some dish towels, and sheets for the bed.

The precious linen was laid away in the shiny black chest. "Till spring," Mama told the girls. "Then we'll wash them and spread them out on the grass to dry, and you'll see how the sun will turn every piece a creamy white. We'll have fine new linen to take with us to America," she finished with a pleased expression.

The next get-together occurred several weeks later. Mama brought from the storage room the bags full of goose feathers collected over the summer.

"Oh, good!" Gisella clapped her hands. "We're having a feather-picking party tonight!"

"Yes," Mama nodded. "I'd better get busy and prepare something extra special for the women." She bustled about happily, and in a little while, the house was full of the most appetizing smells.

Promptly at five the women arrived. "Umm, umm!" Muncie Neni sniffed appreciatively. "What smells so good here?"

"Stuffed cabbage?" Zali Neni cried.

"Naturally," Mama replied with a laugh. "It's my best recipe."

Muncie Neni smacked her lips. "So let's get to work everybody," she ordered. "The sooner we do, the sooner we eat."

They seated themselves in a circle, each with a bag of feathers beside her. Dipping into the bag, each woman scooped up a handful of feathers and dropped them into the lap of her apron. Holding one feather at a time, she stripped the feathery fringe from the central rib and deposited it in a large sack in the center of the circle. The skeleton

119

rib was tossed aside into a large pot.

As Gisella worked away at her sack of feathers, she found herself thinking about how useful geese are. Their meat was good to eat, rendered goose fat was delicious for frying or spread on bread, people used their soft down and feathers for filling pillows and warm puffy quilts. Gisella's mind wandered back to last summer when Mama and Szerena had carefully plucked the down from the backs and chests of the geese. Afterward, the geese floundered about pink-skinned and naked-looking. Did it hurt them? Mama said no. Still they squawked indignantly while it was being done. They acted so uncomfortable, as if they were ashamed to be parading around without any clothes. Of course, it didn't take very long before they were all covered again with fresh down, and then she was glad. The new growth felt even softer and fluffier than the old.

Szerena broke into her thoughts. "Careful! Don't mix in any of the ribs. They belong in the pot!"

By now, wisps of fluff were floating all over the house. They tickled nostrils, swam into open mouths and eyes, and settled down on hair and clothing like fresh snow. At the end of about an hour of this, Mama called a halt. "Time to eat!"

Bags, sacks, and pot were quickly pushed aside. Aprons were shaken free of feathery tufts. In a jiffy, the table was set, and Mama ladled out portions of steaming sweet-and-sour cabbage rolls.

In the midst of all the gay banter, the door suddenly opened, and in marched Andros with his zither tucked under his arm.

"Hah. Leave it to Andros!" Zali Neni cried. "He knows the right time to come!"

"Of course!" Andros agreed with a grin, seating himself at the table. "I could smell that delicious cabbage all the way from home." He shoveled a big forkful into his mouth. "Oh, is this good!" he grunted. "The rice and meat stuffing is light and tender. Not heavy, like my mother-in-law's." He winked at Mama. "Maybe the secret is that you have put some of this light, fluffy down and feathers in your stuffed cabbage. No?"

There were bursts of laughter from all.

Gisella and Szerena ate with relish, too. Such a feast! Excepting for the Sabbath, when Mama always managed to provide chicken or goose, meat seldom appeared on their table.

Now glasses of hot tea were served. And lastly, dried kernels of corn that had been boiled in sweetened water. Gisella and Szerena dearly loved this confection. When Mama poured a small mound into their palms, they fell upon the sugared morsels until not a speck was left.

The meal over, Gisella and Szerena cleared away the dishes, while the women resumed their work. Andros set his zither across his knees and began strumming. He played a quick succession of merry tunes, rollicking dances, and love songs. The entire group joined in the choruses, singing at the top of their voices.

As the jolly evening progressed, the big sack grew bulkier and bulkier. Soon it was bedtime for Gisella. She curled up contentedly under the covers, while all around her the feather-picking bee continued. Despite the lively conversation and music, she drifted off into sleep.

All of a sudden she was jarred awake! For a moment she lay still, wondering what had happened. Was the party over? It must be. The room was dark. . . . Then what had aroused her? The answer came from the barn — excited cacklings and squawkings, the insistent mooing of the cow! What was all the commotion about?

Gisella's toes moved gently to touch Szerena, but her hand reaching out for Mama found only emptiness.

"What's the matter?" Szerena asked, her voice heavy with sleep.

"Where's Mama?" Gisella asked. "Mama!" she called out into the darkness.

Szerena bolted upright. "Mama's not here!" she cried. "What's all that noise from the barn?"

"I don't know."

They could hear boots crunching on the snow. The door burst open, and a rush of icy air swept in. "Mama?" the sisters whispered.

"Yes."

"What is it, Mama? What's the matter?"

"It's a fox. He must have gotten through a loose board of the barn, and he's after our fowl. I struck at him with a broom, but I couldn't chase him out. I'm going across the street to get Mari's father. Szerena, throw on your coat. Take the broom and bang away at the side of the barn till we get back. Gisella, you stay in bed!"

In a flash, Szerena was in her coat and boots and running toward the barn. Gisella sprang from the bed, pushed aside the curtain, and pressed her nose against the cold glass.

The moon shone silvery white on the soft snow. Gisella could clearly follow the animal's tracks which made a path toward the barn. She could see Szerena whacking away furiously with the broom. From inside the barn, the clamor rose to a terrifying crescendo. "Oh, the poor things!" Gisella cried, hopping up and down. "What's taking Mari's father so long?"

The minutes crept by. Gisella shivered with excitement and cold. At last she heard stomping, and a burly figure bundled in a shaggy sheepskin coat stood outlined in the moonlight. It was Mari's father, Yena, and he had a long gun in his hand. Close behind him was Mama swinging a lamp.

"All right, Szerena," Mama shouted. "Stop the banging and give me the broom. Get inside the house. I'm going into the barn to drive the fox out."

Mama pushed open the door of the barn. As she did so, a gray shadow streaked past her. Swiftly it flew across the snow.

Yena Bacsi raised his gun and took aim. Bang! The shot whipped across the air and rolled into the distant hills. Something feathery dropped from the fox's jaws.

Again the gun exploded. Bang! This time the fox somersaulted in midair, fell, and was still!

Yena Bacsi approached and stared down at the mangled chicken. He turned the dead fox over with his boot. "Well, this one won't be stealing any more of our fowl," he said. Slinging the gun over his shoulder, he grabbed hold of the fox's tail and started for home dragging the animal behind him. "Good night!" he called.

"Good night, Yena," Mama returned, "and we thank you."

Szerena and Gisella were waiting at the door as Mama came in. "Oh, Mama," they squealed, "we saw the whole thing! It was awful!"

"Well, it's over now. Back into bed, the two of you, or you'll catch your death of cold."

They needed no urging. They bounded into bed and snuggled under the warm quilt.

"Can you imagine that fox!" Gisella said to Szerena. "He certainly was bold, coming right to our very door!"

"He was probably hungry," replied Szerena. "It's been so freezing cold these last weeks, the wild animals haven't been able to find any food for themselves. Mama," she asked, "what is Yena Bacsi going to do with the fox's fur?"

"Sell it, I guess."

"But you can get a lot of money for fox fur."

"It rightfully belongs to Yena Bacsi. He shot it."

"Oh, Mama," Gisella cried, "what if that fox had bitten you? He's got very sharp teeth!"

"An old hen like me?" Mama said, laughing. "When he had a whole barn full of young chickens to choose from?"

TWELVE

W

INTER'S PENDULUM swung so slowly,
time seemed suspended over the frozen landscape.
But letters from Papa were coming more frequently.
Early in February, a letter arrived which made departure from Helmecz suddenly very real.

> . . . . *I have booked your passage on the*
> S.S. Rotterdam, *leaving from the city of Rot-*
> *terdam, in Holland, on May 5th. I do not*
> *know exactly how long it takes to get to Rot-*
> *terdam from Helmecz, but to be on the safe*
> *side, you should leave at least a week or so*
> *before so that you will be there in ample*
> *time.*

126

I think that Jozsi's offer for the farm is a
fair one and I approve completely. He is a
good man, hard-working and honest. With
your sister Zali's help, and the help of their
three sons, they will keep the farm going.

As far as the household goods are con-
cerned, sell whatever you can. Take only
what you feel you cannot bear to part with.
Remember, you can get everything right here
in America.

Now that the time is drawing near, I am
very impatient. I cross off each day on the
calendar with a prayer.

Kiss the children for me. All my love.
Herschel

We won't really go, Gisella kept telling herself. At the very last minute, something will happen. Maybe Mama will decide that she doesn't want to leave Helmecz after all. Maybe Papa will come here instead.

She tried once to convey her unhappiness to Szerena. But sensible Szerena brushed her arguments aside. "We're going to join our papa in a new and wonderful land. So you might just as well get used to the idea."

After that, Gisella kept her feelings to herself.

"To get into America," Papa had written, "it's not necessary for you to know how to read and write." But in Ungwar, Mama learned that in order to leave the country, she would have to sign her name to get an exit permit.

"I don't know how to sign my name," Mama said with dismay. "I was never taught how."

The official was polite but firm. "I'm sorry. The papers must be signed by the person leaving."

"Never mind, Mama," Szerena whispered. "We'll teach you how. There's nothing to it. You'll learn. You'll see."

That evening, when the supper dishes were cleared away, the lessons began. Gisella gave Mama her slate and a fresh piece of chalk. Szerena wrote Mama's full name in big letters on a sheet of paper torn from her copybook. In the glow of the oil lamp, Mama sat bent over the slate, clutching the chalk tightly as Szerena guided her hand. Slowly and painfully they worked away trying to copy the letters.

By the end of the week, Mama was shaking her head despairingly. "It's no use! I'll never learn!"

For a moment, Gisella felt a surge of hope. Perhaps we won't be able to go! But when she saw the distress in Mama's face, she felt ashamed. "Mama, you've almost got the first part," she encouraged. "All you need is a little more practice, and you'll be able to write the rest."

Mama's smile was rueful. "The children are now teaching their mother," she remarked. She regarded her toil-worn fingers. "It's odd. These hands can milk a cow and spin and weave. They

128

can knit and crochet and do so many more things. Yet when it comes to shaping some simple letters, they are suddenly clumsy." She sighed and picked up the chalk. "You see, children, how important it is to get an education when you're young? When one is grown-up, it is very difficult to learn. I thank God we're going to America. There, at least, you'll be able to go on with your learning."

With patience and practice, Mama succeeded. A week later Mama returned to the bureau in Ungwar.

The official handed Mama a paper. "Sign here," he said brusquely.

Mama took a deep breath and picked up the pen.

"Don't be nervous," Szerena said quietly. "Write just the way you did when we practiced at home."

Mama bent over the important-looking document. Her mouth screwed up with the effort as slowly, but steadily, she formed the letters of her name.

"There!" Putting the pen down with a flourish, she straightened up, smiling triumphantly.

Stamp! Stamp! The official fixed the date, folded the document, and turned it over to Mama. There was nothing more to deter them from leaving Helmecz.

Early spring sunshine spread pale and thin

across the land. Snow that had shrouded the village for so long suddenly slithered with a rushing sound from the rooftops and ran in icy rivulets down the hilly streets. It was wonderful to smell the earth again, to see the bark of the trees subtly change color as they quickened to life. It was wonderful to feel an occasional promise of warmth in the air.

Always before, Gisella had welcomed the coming of spring. No more frozen drinking water or frostbitten fingers and toes. No more having to bring in washed garments hardened into weird shapes so stiff they could stand alone. But now she wished only that she could hold back the days that followed relentlessly one upon the other.

"I can't put off selling our things any longer," Mama remarked one morning.

"But, Mama, we're not leaving for two weeks," Szerena protested. "What'll we use in the meantime?"

"The people that buy them won't take them away till we're ready to leave." Mama's eyes roamed the room. "There's so much to get rid of," she added with a hint of sadness.

The very next day people started coming. One man purchased all the grain and the livestock. The Salomon family took all the furniture and Papa's books.

"Why can't we at least bring Papa his books?" Gisella asked Szerena.

"Don't you remember? We wrote and asked

Papa what we should do about them, and he said to sell them. In America, he said, you can borrow all the books you need, and it doesn't cost you anything."

The draperies, the dishes, and most of the cooking utensils Mama was leaving for Zali Neni. The ax and some other farm implements would go to Imre. Odds and ends Mama intended to distribute among their many other friends in the village. It was strange, Gisella thought, how all the dear familiar things that have lived with you your whole life could be disposed of so quickly and matter-of-factly.

The last days were a hurly-burly of packing, while in between, neighbors kept dropping in to wish the family Godspeed. "Don't forget," they said, "you must write and tell us how everything really is." Over and over Mama and the girls had to promise they would.

The day before departure finally arrived. Clothing, Mama's fine linen, the good china and silverware, as well as some special copper pots, and the beautiful brass candlesticks handed down from Great-grandma, were all tied up in table-cloths and bed sheets. The bulky bundles stood around the room like sleeping ghosts waiting for the morrow. In the morning still another bundle would be added, for the bed would be stripped and the bedding packed for the journey.

By sundown, there was no more to do. Mama

131

took her girls by the hand. Silently they walked out into the twilight and sat down on the ledge. No one spoke.

Still shadows tinged with blue, heralding evening, began their slow descent. Gisella thought, at this very moment, our cow has fallen asleep in a strange barn. The chickens are roosting on someone else's rafters. They're blinking their eyes as if nothing has happened. And the geese — I wonder how they really feel in their new home?

When the first star appeared, Mama broke the silence. "We'd better go to bed, children. We have to be up before the sun tomorrow."

THIRTEEN

THE MORNING SKY was already streaked with pale green when Bacsi Jozsi drove up in his wagon with Yena and Kalman. Behind them, in a buggy borrowed from a neighbor, came Zali Neni and Sandor.

Gisella had never ridden in a buggy. How splendid it looked with its spirited dusky-brown horse! Well, she'd be leaving Helmecz in handsome style, anyway.

Bacsi Jozsi scrambled down from his perch. "Come, boys," he said, "let's get at the bundles right away. They have to catch a train you know."

Numbly Gisella stood beside Szerena watching their possessions being loaded on the wagon. There

133

was a heavy weight on her chest; it made her want to sigh with every breath.

Zali Neni's arm was around Mama. Her usually jolly face was expressionless, but her eyes, like Mama's, were grief-stricken. They're sisters, Gisella thought. Just like me and Szerena! Only I never thought of them that way before. Even though Szerena and I quarrel sometimes, still, if we had to be separated, perhaps never to see each other again, I couldn't bear it! Her eyes misted. Quickly she turned away.

The new grass was just beginning to shoot up all around the house. In the orchard, the trees were already in bud. Beyond lay the fields where the idle ground waited to be turned. This was home! I'll never forget you! Never! No matter how far away they take me. I'll remember you always!

"Gisella, it's time to go," Mama called softly. "You'll sit with me in the wagon. Szerena, you go in the buggy with Sandor."

Gisella stared fixedly at Mama. A gust of anger tore through her pent-up misery. "No!" she screamed. "I won't ride in the wagon! I want to ride in the buggy! No! No! No!"

In a fury, she stamped her feet, and her fists flailed the air. "I don't want to ride in the wagon! I don't want to leave here! This is my home! I don't want to!"

Bacsi Jozsi and Zali Neni exchanged unhappy glances, while the boys, abashed by the unexpected outburst, tried not to look at Gisella. Mama reached out toward her, but Gisella's rage left her as suddenly as it had come. A gulping sob broke from her throat, and the tears rolled down her cheeks. She buried her head in Mama's skirt.

"Please, Gisella," Szerena pleaded tearfully. "You can ride in the buggy if you want. I don't mind going in the wagon."

Bacsi Jozsi drew a handkerchief from his pocket and blew hard. "Well now, I guess everything's ready," he said with a great show of heartiness. "Come along, Gisella. Up you go!" He swung her high and plunked her down in the buggy beside Sandor. She looked so woebegone with her pale, tear-streaked face, her small frame shaken by an occasional sob, that Sandor felt a tightness in his own throat. "Giddap!" he yelled brusquely.

The buggy moved off. Up ahead lumbered the wagon with Mama, Szerena, and Zali Neni up front with Bacsi Jozsi; Yena and Kalman sat on the bundles in the rear. As they turned off their street into the main thoroughfare, they came upon a sturdy figure standing in the middle of the road, arms outstretched. It was Imre! "Hold on there!" he shouted. "You haven't said good-bye to me!"

The horses reined to a stop.

"Imre!" Szerena cried. "We thought you had forgotten about us!"

"What? And let you go off without even saying good riddance?"

With a bound he was up on the wagon ledge.
"I want to thank you for all the wonderful tools
you left me," he said to Mama. "Good-bye and
I wish all of you good luck in the new world."

"Good-bye, Imre. God bless you."

Imre pressed a small bar of chocolate into Szerena's hand. "To sweeten the journey," he said,
and he jumped off.

Next he ran to the buggy. He gazed up into
Gisella's mournful face. "Don't feel so bad, little
girl," he said gently. "You know, someday I'll be
coming to America, too."

Gisella's eyes opened wide. "You will?"

He nodded. "Yes. Sooner than you think. I'll
prove it to you. Hold out your hand!" he ordered.
He placed a shining gold button in her palm. "You
hold on to that. It's one of the buttons of my
sainted father's army uniform. When I get to
America, the first thing I'll do is find you and ask
you to give it back. Agreed?"

Gisella took a deep breath. She squeezed the
button tight in her fist. Imre had made her feel
so much better.

"And now, let's have a great big smile for a
going away present," he coaxed.

It took a moment, but the smile did appear —
a bit forlorn but definitely a smile.

"Well," Imre smiled approvingly, "that's the
way I want to remember you."

The buggy rolled on. Gisella kept looking

136

backward at Imre till he was lost to sight. Slowly she uncurled the fingers of her hand and stared down at the button.

The big locomotive stood puffing in the station. Hurriedly Bacsi Jozsi and the boys unloaded the possessions into the baggage car.

Zali Neni clung to Mama for a long while. "Maybe, if you find life good in America, we'll come also," she said.

The engine bell sounded a warning clang. "All aboard!" the conductors shouted.

"Good-bye! Good-bye, my darlings! Oh, how I'm going to miss you!" Zali Neni's voice choked up as she hugged the girls to her ample bosom.

The boys gathered around, shook the girls' hands, and let themselves be kissed. Bacsi Jozsi put his arm around Mama's shoulder. "A good safe journey. God bless you and watch over all of you!"

Through the blur of farewells, Gisella caught a glimpse of Kalman's face. It looked crumpled up. Was he going to cry? She put her hands to her face and felt the wetness of her own tears.

"All aboard!" The command was insistent.

"Come. Come! Enough already! They have to go!" Bacsi Jozsi ordered in a husky voice. Hastily he herded Mama and the girls up the steep iron steps of the train.

With a sudden jerk, the train began to slide slowly along the station. With noses pressed against the window, the girls stared out at their relatives waving farewell from below. Zali Neni was crying openly, and Bacsi Jozsi was trying to comfort her.

Clackety-clack — the train rolled relentlessly forward, cutting them adrift. Anxious eyes strained to catch a last glimpse of the dear familiar faces.

The swaying train rushed determinedly onward. For a long time the family sat without speaking, each locked in her own sadness. Occasionally Gisella's gaze drifted toward the window. They were hurtling by unending stretches of open land. The world was so vast! She hadn't realized it before. Never in her whole life had she been beyond Ungwar, and now she was being thrust into a great big wide world — and everywhere people were living and working, and she had never even thought about them.

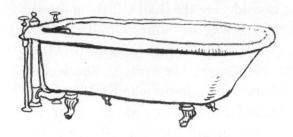

FOURTEEN

THE HOURS crawled by slowly. Wearied of sitting still, the girls roamed up and down the narrow corridor outside the compartment. Occasionally some fellow passenger addressed a few words to them, but they were too shy to respond with more than smiles.

Eventually the sun sank, and gray dusk settled down onto the landscape. "It's too dark to see out," Szerena said, "and anyway, I'm hungry."

"Me too," echoed Gisella.

"All right then," Mama said. From her basket, she took pieces of roast goose and slices of black bread liberally spread with white goose fat, salt, and paprika. It tasted so good!

The long bewildering day had left them utterly spent. Even talking was an effort. Gisella put her head in Mama's lap and promptly fell asleep. Much later a sudden jolt jogged her awake. She looked around in the darkness, half-stupefied. Where was she? All the lights had been turned off, except for a small one burning in the corridor. She saw that Mama and Szerena, like everyone else, were sleeping sitting up. Reassured, she dropped off to sleep again.

By the second day, they were extremely weary of the endless motion, the monotonous clacking of the train wheels, the cramped quarters. Their stomachs had begun to rebel against the dry cold food. They felt gritty and unclean in their rumpled clothes. Unable to stretch out, sleep was fitful. Their bodies were stiff and sore, and their eyes burned. The girls slumped listlessly in their seats, no longer interested in the ever-changing scenery flashing by the window.

"Aren't we ever going to get off this train?" whined Gisella.

"Just one more night," Mama promised. The strain showed in her pale face also.

"Pr-a-gue! Next stop, Pra-a-gue!"

Instantly faces brightened. Passengers bestirred themselves, collected their bundles and packages, and slipped into coats and jackets.

"We'll be changing trains here," Mama said.

"Oh, not another train!" Szerena complained.

"Yes, another train to Dresden and then still another one to Rotterdam. The trains are slow, and they stop so often. Papa was right when he said we should allow a week. But we have a couple of hours to wait now. That will give us a chance to stretch our legs, and we'll be able to see something of Prague."

The girls clung close to Mama as she elbowed her way through the crowded railway station and out into the wide streets. They stared round-eyed at the tall buildings — some of them were four stories high and made of brick and stone! Nevertheless, to eyes accustomed to the vivid colors of the countryside, the city presented a dull leaden aspect. It was Gisella who voiced what they were thinking. "Everything looks so gray!"

Szerena's head ached, and she had such a dreadful wanting-to-throw-up feeling. "I hate trains!" she said. "I wish we didn't have to ride on another one."

Just then they heard a resounding clang! clang!

"Look," Gisella pointed, "a train running right in the middle of the street!"

They stood fascinated, watching it roll along two iron tracks imbedded in the road. From the top of the train, a long pole slid along an overhead wire. Blue electric sparks sputtered and crackled as the wheel on top of the pole moved along the wire.

"Can you imagine! A street train!" Szerena cried.

"I've heard people talk about them," Mama said. "They're called trolley cars."

"Mama, I don't want to walk anymore," Gisella said suddenly. "I don't feel good."

"Me, neither," added Szerena.

Mama looked down at their faces which had taken on a yellowish-greenish color. "What you children need is something to settle your stomachs," she said anxiously. Her eyes combed the area. "Come," she coaxed and led them into a small cafe.

It was dim and cool and quiet inside. They slumped into chairs at a marble-topped table, while the cafe owner brought them each a foaming glass of beer.

"Drink it all up," Mama ordered.

"Ugh! It's bitter!" Gisella cried, making a face.

"Sour!" Szerena cried.

"Never mind the taste! Just drink!"

The beer was cool, but it seemed to warm up their stomachs. Szerena exclaimed about the bubbles running up her nose, but gradually the uncomfortable feeling in their stomachs went away.

At last, surrounded by their belongings, the family stood as if lost amidst the milling throng in the Rotterdam station. Even strong, self-reliant Mama seemed uncertain, as hand to mouth, she looked around worriedly.

A well-dressed man, wearing eyeglasses, approached and addressed Mama in a foreign tongue. She shook her head. Smiling, he then asked in Hungarian, "Is there someone coming to meet you?"

"No. We know no one here," Mama replied. "We're sailing for America in a couple of days."

The man nodded. "Have you a place to stay meanwhile?"

"No — not yet. . . ." Mama hesitated. "I was going to look for one. . . ."

"Well, then, perhaps I can be of some help. First, however, permit me to introduce myself. I am Mr. Vogel. I own a modest hotel not far from here. Many people going to America stop at my place. It's clean and quiet. And our rates are reasonable. If you like, I can take you there."

"Oh, thank you. Thank you very much." Mama was plainly relieved. "Could we go right away? The children are worn out. They need to rest."

"Of course. My porter will take care of your things." He beckoned a young boy who then came running. "Permit me." He took Mama's arm and smiled encouragingly at the girls. "It's not far."

Their first fleeting impression of Rotterdam was of narrow houses set close together, cobblestoned streets, and many bicycles. Before long they arrived at a small hotel.

Wearily they trailed behind Mr. Vogel along a wide hallway. He stopped at a numbered door, turned the key in the lock, and waved them into a

143

large spotlessly clean room with two beds.

"Is this satisfactory?" he asked.

"Oh, yes. Very," Mama replied.

"Good. I'll have your things brought right up." Mr. Vogel paused at the door. "Perhaps you'd like a little supper?"

Mama shook her head. "No, thank you. We're not hungry. We're much too tired."

"I understand. Have a good night's rest." He bowed himself out.

It was heavenly being able to stretch out full length on a real bed! Long before Mama had finished putting things in order, both girls were sound asleep.

The hotel was a fascinating place, filled with so many things they had never seen before.

For instance, the broad carpeted stairway. No one in all Helmecz lived in a house with a staircase leading to another floor. Nobody even had second floors. They delighted in the luxurious feeling of sinking down into the thick, patterned carpeting on the stairs. "I wish there were lots more steps," Gisella cried. At every opportunity she went tripping up and down the stairs, just for the sheer joy of it.

Then there was the bathroom. "Imagine!" Szerena said. "All you have to do is pull a chain, and all that water comes rushing out! I wonder where it comes from?"

And they flushed the toilet over and over just to see the water burst forth in a torrent and then magically disappear.

To one side was an enormous tub. "Did you ever see anything so shiny clean and smooth?" exclaimed Gisella. "It stands on little legs! What's it for?"

"For bathing," Mama explained.

Taking a bath in Helmecz had always been a chore. First you had to heat lots of water on top of the stove. Then you carried it and poured it into a large round zinc tub. In no time, the water would cool, and Mama had to keep bringing more hot water. But here, one simply turned on a faucet.

Mama's hand reached under the faucet. "It's like a hot fountain," she said, laughing in wonder and delight.

In the lobby downstairs, the wall facing the street was all glass windows. Here they sat a good part of the day looking out on the busy tree-shaded street and observing the passersby.

"Everyone in Rotterdam is so well-dressed! Even the children!" Gisella commented.

Szerena replied, "I guess they're all rich."

Once they saw a little girl gliding by as if she were floating, her blond pigtails streaming behind her. How could that be? They rushed forward for a better look.

"She has something strapped on her shoes!" cried Gisella.

"Wheels!" Szerena added. "She's got wheels attached to her shoes! It's like riding in a wagon."

Mr. Vogel overheard. "Only you're your own wagon," he put in, laughing. "They're roller skates."

They stared up at him, puzzled.

"You mean to say you've never heard of roller skates?"

They shook their heads.

It was Mr. Vogel's turn to look puzzled. "My, my!" he murmured.

"Mr. Vogel, do they have roller skates in America?" Gisella asked hopefully.

"Oh, yes! Lots of them!"

The sisters grinned at each other happily.

The day before sailing, a notice arrived from the U.S. Health Officer requesting the family to appear for a physical examination.

"Why do we need to do that?" asked Gisella.

"Well, they have to be very careful," Mama answered. "They don't want any contagious sicknesses brought into their country."

"They won't shave our heads, will they?" Szerena queried in alarm.

Gisella stared at her. "Shave our heads?" she repeated.

"Don't you remember, Mama?" Szerena went on. "There was that woman in Helmecz. Oh, you know. The wife of the cattle dealer. She was always so proud of her hair. It *was* beautiful, thick and black and so long she could sit on it. But she wasn't very clean. And then we heard that they found lice in her hair. So they shaved her whole head before they would let her go on the ship."

Gisella covered her head with her hands. "I don't want them to cut off my hair!"

"Nobody's going to cut off your hair. Stop worrying," Mama said.

Nevertheless, that night, all three washed their hair and fine-combed it over and over just to make sure.

The following morning, Mr. Vogel guided them through the streets to one of the numerous canals crisscrossing the city. There they boarded a long, white boat and found seats on deck among the other passengers.

Toot! Toot! Slowly the boat moved away from the dock. The sisters clung nervously to their seats. "They've never been on a boat before," Mama explained.

"It's perfectly safe," Mr. Vogel assured them.

The boat slipped smoothly over the grayish-green water past row on row of narrow-roofed houses lining both sides of the canal.

"This is really a part of the sea you're traveling on," Mr. Vogel commented. "It runs into the harbor and joins the ocean."

"The Atlantic Ocean," Szerena added.

By the time they had reached their destination, both girls were agreed that if crossing the Atlantic

147

were half as pleasant, they were in for a good time.

The health office was spacious and white and spotlessly clean. At the reception desk, a middle-aged, motherly-looking woman spoke to Mama in their own language. "You and the children come with me," she said.

Her voice and manner were reassuring. None the less, Gisella and Szerena held fast to Mama's hand.

"It is required that you bathe before the doctor's examination," the woman stated as she opened the door. "The children can have their bath in here, and Mother can use the one just across the hall."

Separating from Mama in this strange place! Panic descended upon Gisella. Szerena, too, shook her head emphatically, crying, "No, no!" Desperately they clung to Mama.

"It's all right," the woman said soothingly. "You can all bathe in the same room if you like." As she left, she handed Mama some white dressing gowns and said, "Put these on afterward for the doctor's examination."

The room was warm and steamy. Quickly they undressed and climbed into the tub. Soon all three were splashing away contentedly.

Bath over, they donned the gowns and were conducted to the doctor's office. The examination was brief but thorough. Next they were turned over to a nurse. Sure enough, she promptly began parting their hair and inspecting their heads closely.

Gisella smiled up at the nurse happily. "We're not like that cattle dealer's wife in Helmecz," she declared, drawing herself up proudly.

"What?" The nurse looked completely mystified.

Mama interrupted quickly. "Oh, she's just talking about some acquaintances in our town."

The nurse's checkup marked the end of the physical examination. Mama was relieved to learn that they had been given a clean bill of health. "Now there's nothing more to do except board the boat," she told the girls.

FIFTEEN

THE GIANT SHIP curved upward alongside the dock, its many colored flags flapping in the breeze, and white steam hissing from one of its large funnels. On the pier, people were laughing, crying, embracing, and talking in many languages.

Gisella felt excited but bewildered as she tried to take in everything. Above the tumult, she heard Mama say, "Good-bye, Mr. Vogel. How can I ever thank you for all your kindness?"

"God be with you and the dear children," he replied. "May you arrive safely in the New World."

At the gangplank, a uniformed guard waved them aboard. A porter led them down many stairs and bewildering lanes of corridors till at last he halted before their cabin.

"It's so tiny!" Szerena cried as they entered. "Like a doll's house!"

"Look at the beds!" Gisella added. "They look like shelves, one on top of the other. I want to sleep on the top one."

Szerena made no protest. She was examining a row of mysterious buttons protruding from the wall near the door. She could not understand the words printed above each button. She pressed one lightly. It slid right into the wall. Gingerly she pushed the others, waiting for something to happen. Nothing did, so she turned to help Mama stow their things away.

A few moments later someone knocked. The door opened, and there stood a stewardess. Behind her was a steward and a ship's officer. "What can we do for you?" they chorused politely.

Mama and the girls looked at one another blankly. The officer pointed to the buttons. "You rang for all of us," he said.

Red-faced and embarrassed, Mama finally managed to say, "Please, excuse . . . I wanted . . . would you . . . could you bring an orange for each child?"

"Certainly, Madam," the officer said. Then he explained what each button was for.

A hoarse blast of sound interrupted them. The room began to vibrate. "We're moving!" Szerena shouted.

"Come along with me," the officer said, "and I'll guide you to the deck, so you can see what's going on."

The deck was jammed with passengers waving handkerchiefs and yelling farewells in many languages. The children, with Mama close behind, made their way through the crowd until they reached the rail.

Looking down, they watched two little tugs pulling and straining at the huge ship moving slowly away from the dock. Above them, screaming sea gulls wheeled about madly as the gap between land and ship grew wider.

Soon the tugs had departed. The gulls abandoned them, too. They were sailing out of the harbor into the open sea. Gradually the passengers drifted away, but Mama and the girls still lingered at the rail. The wind smelled of salt and tar. It whipped past their faces and tugged at strands of their hair. Behind them the greenish water fanned out in a trail of foaming, churning white. The land was fast disappearing. Helmecz seemed so very far away, Gisella realized with a pang. No chance of turning back now — not ever!

"Come," Mama finally spoke. "Let's look around."

Hand in hand they roamed the decks marveling at all they saw. Folding chairs that opened out so one could stretch out on them, lifeboats dangling along the sides, tremendous salons with ornate decorations, carpeted floors, and deep comfortable sofas — and everywhere staircases leading up and down. "You'd never know by looking at the boat from the outside, how big it is on the inside," Szerena exclaimed.

After a few days, however, the novelty of shipboard life wore off. There was always the same limited area in which to promenade. And as far as the eye could see, there was nothing save the monotony of endless water and open sky. There were a number of other families with children on board — Americans. They seemed to be having such a good time romping and laughing together. Unable to make themselves understood, Gisella and Szerena sat on the sidelines watching them enviously.

"I wonder what will happen to us in America?" Gisella said. "Aren't you a little scared, Szerena?"

"I don't know. Everything is bound to be different."

Gisella's voice quavered. "We won't be able to understand a thing anyone says."

"Don't worry. We'll learn."

"Szerena's right," Mama reassured her. "You'll learn fast, you'll see. And don't forget we'll have Papa to help us."

The continuous pitching and rolling of the vessel soon began to make people sick. By the fourth day, both Mama and Gisella lay in their bunk beds with no wish to stir.

"You both missed such a marvelous breakfast. Aren't you at least coming to lunch?" Szerena asked.

Gisella groaned and turned her face toward the wall. "I don't want anything. I feel miserable."

"You go alone," suggested Mama.

"Shall I bring you something?"

"No."

So again Szerena took off by herself. To her surprise, the dining room was half empty. Lots more people must be feeling sick, she decided. Well, it's too bad for them, but it was nice that she could enjoy all this wonderful food. She ate with enjoyment, and the obliging waiter kept plying her with more. Full to the brim and humming contentedly, she made her way back to the cabin.

"Oh, what you missed!" she raved. "I had the most delicious dessert! It was something creamy-smooth and sweet. It's hard to describe, but you eat it with a spoon, and it's icy cold. The waiter called it ice cream. And when he saw how much I liked it, he brought me a second portion. It's the best thing I ever tasted in my whole life!"

Szerena stayed in the cabin for a while, but it was quite evident neither Mama nor Gisella felt like talking. They just lay there with closed eyes ignoring her. There was nothing to do but leave them alone.

Up on deck, the usual groups of romping children were absent. Most of the deck chairs were empty, too. What's happened to everyone? Szerena wondered. She wandered about, balancing herself against the swaying of the vessel.

At dinner, there were even fewer people. Szerena seemed to be the only youngster present. With so few to serve, the waiters hovered over her. She enjoyed their attention almost as much as she did the meal. She ate enormously and with great relish.

"Mama, aren't you and Gisella going to eat something?" she asked sympathetically when she returned. "How about some hot tea or soup or something? Maybe that would make you feel better."

Mama shook her head weakly. "No. Not a thing. I couldn't keep it down. Maybe tomorrow. The stewardess says it comes from the rocking of the boat. After we've had a good night's rest, maybe we'll feel better."

But by morning, neither Mama nor Gisella were any better, and Szerena breakfasted alone. The dining room was practically deserted. Szerena couldn't bear seeing all that appetizing food going to waste, so she ate and ate and ate.

Afterward she ventured outside, but the decks stretched out before her, empty and forlorn. Walking was difficult, for the wind had risen. Overhead, gray-black storm clouds were gathering in an ominous mass. There's no one to even smile at, thought Szerena, feeling suddenly very lonely.

Then something strange started to happen. Was it her imagination, or was the ship rolling more than usual? A queer heavy lump settled itself in her throat. It wouldn't go down, and it refused to come up. It was a peculiar sensation, sort of queasy. Maybe it was from all that food. Ugh! She wished now she hadn't made such a pig of herself.

All of a sudden, the lump rose violently and spilled over the rails into the ocean. For some minutes, she stood there while her insides seemed to be emptying out. Then, shaken and nauseated, she staggered down the stairs to their cabin and into her berth.

For two days a savage storm raged. Buffeted mercilessly by wind and sea, the ship lurched and plunged, its wooden fittings creaking loudly in protest. But in the cabin, Mama and both girls were too sick to even know or care.

Gradually, the storm's wrath subsided, and the sea became as smooth as glass. One by one the sick recovered. Pale and wan-looking, they crawled out of their bunks and onto the sun-swept decks. How good it was to be out in the open again!

At last the ship was nearing New York. Mama and the girls stood leaning against the ship's railing. The moon shone brightly on the water. Suddenly it outlined a tall structure which rose from the very depths of the harbor.

"There she is! The Statue of Liberty!" the cry went up.

The ship was approaching rapidly, and Gisella could clearly see the lighted torch held aloft in the lady's hand, its rays reflected on her spiked crown and serene features. She could not help but be caught up in the wild elation of the other passengers.

Mama's face was radiant with the promise of things to come. "America! America, at last!" she kept murmuring, holding the girls close.

"Look! Oh, look, Gisella!" Szerena pointed with awe to the right.

The New York skyline came into view. Immense, squarish buildings piled one on the other, glistening with pin prickles of light, and from their midst, even taller buildings rising upward like slender shafts of light into the black sky.

The immigration inspectors were already aboard when Mama and the girls joined the passengers gathered in the main salon. First the tourists and American citizens were passed through. Then it was the immigrants' turn. In a room just beyond, relatives and friends waited, ready to vouch for and claim the newcomers. An expectant hush spread through the salon.

The roll call began. One after another, happy, excited groups jumped up from their seats as their names were called. "Here!" There were tears and laughter and joyous embraces, and the lucky ones departed.

Time ticked away. The salon was gradually emptying. Where was Papa? Gisella's eyes strained toward the door.

"If Papa doesn't come, will they send us back?" Szerena asked anxiously.

"He'll be here," Mama replied, but her hands kept clasping and unclasping nervously.

Finally all the passengers were gone. Only Mama and the girls were left. At the other end of the room, the inspectors kept glancing in their direction.

"But supposing Papa doesn't come?" Szerena kept insisting. "What will they do then?"

"Just be patient, Szerena," Mama told her resolutely. "He'll come."

The minutes dropped away like water dripping from a leaky faucet. All at once, from across the room, an inspector smiled toward them and called loudly, "Mrs. Landesman and children!"

Mama rushed forward, her documents in her outstretched hand.

A stranger was coming toward them. Someone tall and thin. In the next instant, Mama was enfolded in his arms. Was this Papa? Gisella felt her heart pound. He has green eyes — just like me!

Papa was looking deep into Mama's face. "How you must have worried when you didn't find me here!" he murmured. His voice was rumbly and low. "Your boat was late. A whole day late."

"It was the storm that held us up," Mama said.

"I know. We were told. Everyone was so anxious. I sat around the waiting room all day. Then I went back to see if everything was all right at my

158

fruit stand — I have a man helping me there now — I didn't realize it would take so long to get back. . . ."

"Never mind. It doesn't matter," Mama interrupted between tears and laughter. "Go greet your daughters."

Papa put a broad hand on the shoulder of each child. They stood trembling, gazing up at him.

"My, my!" he cried in astonishment. "What has happened to the two little babies I left behind?" He threw back his head and laughed, and the laughter rumbled joyously through the room.

As Papa caught them both in his strong arms, the girls buried their faces against his dark jacket, too overwhelmed to speak. Gisella thought, Szerena and I aren't orphans with only a Mama to love, anymore. We're a real family now — a family with a mama *and* a papa.

Papa knelt down and tipped Gisella's chin up.

"Papa!" she whispered in shy happiness. "Oh, Papa!"

About the Author

Sydney Taylor was born on the East Side of New York City and lived there until her early teens. After her marriage, she worked as a secretary and joined the Lenox Hill Players, one of the important theater groups at that time.

She became a mother and housewife three years later, when her daughter, Jo, was born. When Jo was seven years old, Mrs. Taylor resumed her creative activity as a teacher of dramatics in a non-profit children's summer camp. Because of the difficulty in finding material suitable for dramatic presentation by her camp groups, she writes and directs her own plays and composes much of the choreography for them.

Mr. and Mrs. Taylor are great travelers, and everywhere they go they make friends with the children. In England, Italy, Israel, Canada, and the United States children have listened enthralled while Mrs. Taylor discussed her books and Mr. Taylor played the recorder.

Sydney Taylor's first book, *All-of-a-Kind Family,* won the Charles W. Follett Award in 1951 and has become a modern classic. It has been followed by *More All-of-a-Kind Family* and *All-of-a-Kind-Family Uptown.* Much has been written in praise of *All-of-a-Kind Family,* but it is best summed up in the words of May Hill Arbuthnot (*Children and Books*) who wrote, "A pleasanter emissary for Jewish culture, religious piety, and family love than these entertaining books could hardly be found." On the tenth anniversary of its publication, *All-of-a-Kind Family* was published in England. Mrs. Taylor has also written *Mr. Barney's Beard* and *The Dog Who Came to Dinner* for younger children.